Praise for *The Door to January*

"Chilling and suspenseful, this paranormal thriller with a touch of romance will keep readers on the edges of their seats."
—*Kirkus Reviews*

"French has crafted a story that will grab readers' attention from the beginning. Teens will be continually drawn into the intrigue through chapters that present alternating time lines. Readers will feel connected to Natalie and her plight of past, present, and future, and though there are supernatural elements to the story, the emotions and feelings are all too real."
—*School Library Journal*

" . . . the slow unraveling of the house's history, the increasing tension around Natalie's flashbacks to a distant crime, and the creepy but pitiable spirits that haunt her all come together to make a spine-tingling tale."
—*Bulletin of the Center for Children's Books*

"French expertly builds tension and dread in masterful fashion in this truly frightening paranormal thriller, weaving the storylines to a climax that will leave readers gasping."
—*IndiePicks* Magazine

Bram Stoker Award
2017 Nominee, Young Adult Novel

THE
DOOR TO
JANUARY

Other titles for young readers from Islandport Press

Finchosaurus
Gail Donovan

What the Wind Can Tell You
Sarah Marie A. Jette

The Five Stones Trilogy
by G. A. Morgan

The Sugar Mountain Snow Ball
by Elizabeth Atkinson

Mercy: The Last New England Vampire
by Sarah L. Thomson

Billy Boy: The Sunday Soldier of the 17th Maine
by Jean Flahive

THE
DOOR TO
JANUARY

GILLIAN FRENCH

ISLANDPORT  PRESS

Islandport Press
PO Box 10
247 Portland Street
Yarmouth, ME 04096
www.islandportpress.com
books@islandportpress.com

ISBN: 978-1-944762-61-2
Library of Congress Control Number: 2017935695

Dean L. Lunt, Publisher
Printed in the USA by Versa Press

For my parents, Jacqueline and Brent Hall, who always believed

CHAPTER 1

The house was a sad thing in the daylight. It sat on a hilltop, a sagging pile of weathered clapboards and crumbling brick, the gutters stuffed with the refuse of many seasons. It had been grand once, a two-and-a-half-story Colonial built facing the harbor; a huge, swaybacked barn sat on the property in its own private ruin.

Natalie and her cousin Teddy left their bikes at the base of the hill and blazed a trail through the brambles to reach the house. Teddy darted off on his own without a word to her and, within minutes, had completely disappeared.

"Watch out for old wells," she called after him.

Natalie reached the front door and stopped to catch her breath. Waist-high weeds shot up around the granite step, and will-o'-the-wisps were everywhere, cottony gray heads waiting for one stiff breeze to scatter them apart. She stared at the tarnished gleam of the knob. How many times had she opened this door in her dreams? Approximately one million and three. So why resist it now? Simple. She was chicken.

"Come on, Teddy, where are you?" She waited, hands on her hips, and then called out over the fields, "Last one inside is a rotten corpse!"

With a scraping sound, the door opened inward. Teddy's elfin face appeared in the gap, fringed by shaggy blond hair, a smudge of dust on one lens of his horn-rimmed glasses.

"You were saying?"

"How'd you get inside?"

"Easy. The back door's open." He studied her. "Scared?"

"Crapping bricks." Natalie took a deep breath. "Let's do it."

As she stepped into the foyer, Natalie's pulse quickened. The stained walls; the bowed center staircase; the dim and dusty corridor to the rear of the house—she knew it all. Had never set foot inside, and yet, she knew it.

"This is it. This is where I go in my dream." She smacked his shoulder. "I told you."

"Come on, most old houses around here probably look like this. Ye Olde Maine Shack." He lifted a long peel of yellowed wallpaper with the toe of his shoe. "Is it this disgusting in your dream? Because I smell mice. And, like . . . dead things."

"*This* is the house, Teddy. Fixed up and nice, but this is the hallway. It's freaky, admit it."

Her gaze drifted to the ceiling. In the dream, a frosted glass globe hung there; now, a hole gaped where the fixture had once been.

"I admit nothing." He sneezed and dug in his pocket for tissues. "Nat. Seriously. My allergies don't need this."

"Okay, okay. I'll make it fast." She rubbed her forehead, thinking, then grabbed his shoulders and steered. "Let's set up in the kitchen. That's where the dream always takes me. End of the hall, on the right."

The kitchen stared back at them, a dingy room with an enamel sink and splintered glass in the cupboard doors. Natalie saw herself reflected in fragments: tall and sturdy, ginger freckles, dark hair curling loose.

She took the digital voice recorder from her pocket and knelt, setting it on the floor with some reverence. She'd been planning this for so many months, imagining how it would be.

Teddy watched from the doorway, his slim arms folded. "You actually think this is going to work, don't you?"

"If it doesn't, then I guess we'll finally know." He raised his brows. She shrugged. "That I'm insane." She pressed the RECORD button, and said, "This is Natalie Rose Payson." Her voice sounded hollow in the silence. "If somebody here is trying to reach me, I'm listening. I want to make contact." A pause. "Just tell me what you want."

The recorder remained, taking down the minutes as they slipped out the back door, shooting each other sidelong glances, their steps going faster and faster until it was a race, both of them pounding down the hill through chest-high weeds. Teddy was on his bike and pedaling down the lane before Natalie even reached her own, and she kicked dust after him.

On its perch, the house settled and grew another day older.

That night, Natalie slept fitfully in her aunt's summerhouse. Above her, foxfire was dancing.

Three small lights rose from her body around one a.m., drifting like sparks. They played tag as Natalie frowned in her sleep. Flash, flash, they swirled around the room, casting patterns, signaling to each other in the darkness. The foxfire was as organic to her as breathing, and as unconscious. They were her silent ushers into the land of dreams, her observers during the day.

In time, they drifted across the room to hover over Natalie, their host, then sank into her chest one by one, glowing briefly against the fabric of her T-shirt before vanishing.

Natalie jerked, her fists bearing down against the mattress. The same nightmare was back. Tonight, with a twist.

She flew, buffeting on cross breezes. Below her, the house seemed to float in a sea of field and forest. Her singular destination. She descended and passed through the front door.

It was snowing inside. Flakes drifted down from the ceiling, glittering in the lamplight. Natalie continued on, past a moon-faced clock, a carved rack with a mirror. From another room, music played softly.

At the end of the corridor, the kitchen doorway glowed. Natalie went in.

China covered every surface. Plates and bowls, teacups and saucers, all brimming with snow, evidence of some Mad Hatter's party. On a woodstove sat a copper kettle. The steam from the spout had hardened into ice.

Slowly, she turned to face a door to her left set with six panes of glass. This was the dream's apex; it always ended here, with her own face staring back from the glass.

But tonight, there was a shift.

As Natalie moved closer to the door, she heard whispers.

Girls' voices hissed around the frame. "Natalie," they said. "Natalie."

She opened the door to blackness colder than the pits of January.

CHAPTER 2

The tourist dad looked at her sullenly. "Look, either you guys have Clamato or you don't. Which is it?"

"I'm not sure," Natalie repeated, and oh God, her eyes were burning. Three hours into her first shift, and she was going to cry. "I'll check."

"Yeah. You do that. Jaeden, for chrissake." He grabbed his son's hand, who'd scrawled crayon from his coloring-page placemat clear across the tabletop. His wife *tsked* and started wiping at the stain with a wet napkin.

Natalie ducked into the kitchen, facing the pantry shelves for a moment so she could close her eyes and breathe, the only remedy she knew for an impending meltdown. She hated being sniped at, she hated being treated like an idiot; so far, waitressing was a blast.

"Ever done anything like this before?"

The punk waitress stood behind her, filling pebbled glasses at the soda fountain. Her name tag read DELIA. She kept her eyes on her work.

"That obvious, huh?"

Of all the things you should never, ever do on your first day of work, Natalie was pretty sure bawling was numero uno. The punk waitress didn't look like she ever bawled. She looked like somebody who stomped bawlers under her 8-eye Dr. Martens.

6

"Hey, I'm not ragging on you. The guy at table five's got that covered, am I right?"

Natalie sniffed, hating herself for it.

"Okay. That's it. Come on."

Delia took her arm and led her through the swinging doors into the dining room of Payson's Grill, all chrome and red leatherette, early American greasy spoon to the letter, complete with locals munching hamburgers at the counter and a jukebox in the back.

Natalie locked eyes with Tourist Dad, across the room. "He hates me."

"He doesn't know you. To him, you're a mule, get it?"

Delia's hair was buzzed close to her scalp, her eyes and skin chocolate-brown. She looked to be a couple of years older than Natalie, eighteen or so, but she was a stranger, no one Natalie remembered from the fun times at Bernier Middle School.

"Listen up. None of this"—she gestured to the Grill at large—"is personal. Mr. Table Five is a jerk, and he'll walk out of your life forever after his predictable slice of blueberry pie à la mode. That's the great thing about waitressing. Fast turnover."

Natalie smiled in spite of herself.

Delia nudged her. "You'll live to serve another table. Cross my heart."

" 'Scuse me, ladies, clear a path." Bess—forties, huge perm, blue mascara—shoved between them with a tray. It was the third time she'd bumped into Natalie since breakfast, and now she even managed to step on her toe.

"Ow! God." Natalie watched the older waitress ram through the kitchen doors. "I'm always in her way."

"Nah." Delia cracked her gum. "She's in yours. Oh, yeah, and heads up: If you land a regular who gives good tips, she'll try to switch tables with you. Just say no. Trust me, you guys aren't destined to be friends anyway."

The cook hollered, "Order up!" through the pickup window and Delia looked at the plates. "It's you. Steak and fries, heavy on the macho."

As Natalie set down his glass of Clamato, Mr. Table Five frowned over his wife's fish chowder. "What, you guys too cheap to give out oyster crackers?"

Natalie headed back to the kitchen. Delia grinned as she passed, and Natalie couldn't help it. She laughed out loud.

Aunt Cilla, Dad's younger sister, was in the manager's office counting the weekly deposit when Natalie looked in on her. Cilla was a large woman, tall and roomy through the chest and hips, her dark curls streaked with premature gray. A pair of wire-rimmed frames balanced on the end of her nose.

It was Cilla's restaurant now, left to her in Grampie's will, but the desk had the same blotter and in/out baskets it had had when Natalie was a kid. The same old photographs hung on the wall—Natalie's late grandparents on opening day twenty years ago, she and Teddy as kids, sitting together at the front counter. That last one struck Natalie—did she really used to be that little girl with the dorktastic pigtails, feet barely able to touch the floor, waiting for Grampie to fix her a milkshake?

Still counting, Cilla glanced up. "Need me out front?"

"I was wondering—should I take my break now? It's past one."

"Oh, jeez, I forgot!" Cilla swept the cash away. "I'll cover your tables." She put her hands on Natalie's shoulders. "How's it been so far? Torture? Wish I could train you myself, but the deposit always takes—"

"No worries. I'm catching on." Training had been practically nonexistent, the old sink-or-swim method.

"Are you okay, hon? Really?"

Natalie smiled wanly. "I didn't get much sleep last night."

"I guess not. Look at that set of baggage under your eyes." Cilla ran her thumbs beneath her niece's lashes. "I'm just so darn pleased to have you here." She chucked Natalie's chin. "Go on. Eat."

After Natalie punched her timecard, she found Delia untying her apron in the kitchen.

"Lunch buddies, huh?" Delia crooked her finger. "Okay, the magical mystery tour continues. Follow."

The cook slapped together two cheeseburgers while Delia drew sodas at the fountain.

"Keep yourself hydrated," Delia said. "Between the ovens and the lobster cooker, it gets mondo hot back here. We don't want anybody fainting."

"Drink a lot. Got it."

They sat on the loading dock together, staring off down the shuttered storefronts of Main Street. Bernier was a fading Maine town, had been ever since the cannery closed ten years ago, leaving much of Hancock County dependent on summer-people dollars.

Delia nudged Natalie's leg. "So. Gimme the dirt. I mean, I know you're Cilla's niece from Lincoln. She's been talking about you coming to stay for the summer since forever. You must really want to earn crummy tips."

Even as Natalie laughed, the nightmare flared again in her mind. Glittering snowflakes. Whispers. A cold so intense it seemed to freeze the air in her lungs. Cue the mundane answer she'd given Cilla and Mom and Dad two months ago when she'd first asked to come here; only Teddy knew the truth, and he was sworn to secrecy.

"I'm saving up for a car. I got my license in May. What about you?"

"Graduated this spring. Taking a year off. My mom's freaking about it, but that's pretty typical." Delia stretched. Her earlobes were lined with silver studs. "You psyched to spend your summer in these"—she laughed—"lush surroundings?"

"It's not so bad. I grew up here. We only moved to Lincoln about two and a half years ago."

"Seriously? Holy ships passing in the night. My family moved here last fall. Wait a sec—you're not saying you actually *missed* living in Bernier?"

Natalie sought out glimpses of the harbor between the shops. "Not exactly." She hesitated, tried to play it off with a smile. "No place like home, I guess."

Quitting time couldn't come soon enough. Bouncing

between tables was impossible—somebody was always flagging Natalie down—and she didn't *know* anything. Could you get the turkey club on rye bread with double coleslaw? How well-done was medium-well? Did they have a wine list? (Oh. That was a joke.) At very long last, shaky and sticky, Natalie said her good-byes, punched out, and made for the front exit, nearly colliding with a boy coming in.

"Sorry." She sidestepped him. Recognition made her turn back, though it'd been over two years and he'd changed a lot. He was looking at her, too.

Tall and lanky, he wore a Red Sox hat over his dark hair, which grew thick and straight to his shoulders. Three moles were scattered across his deeply tanned cheek like drops of ink. His eyes were hazel, hawkish, and fixed on her.

A run-in like this was bound to happen, but she hadn't expected it so soon. Her hands curled into fists. As the moment stretched on, he started to speak, then stopped again, daunted by the expression on her face; frowning, looking almost *wounded*, of all things, he went inside. Natalie caught a final flash of his eyes through the glass pane, glancing back, his brows drawn. Lowell Emerick—so changed, yet so much the same.

She squeezed the handlebars as she biked toward Morning Glory Lane, frustrated by the way her grip shook. Stupid. They didn't scare her anymore, not Lowell or any of the others. And that's what this summer was about, right? Facing things?

But now that January day returned to her in a series of

light-blasted images: Teddy with blood under his nose, his breath crystallizing in the air, tears running down his cheeks. How the muzzle of the gun had slowly traced his jawline and lingered beneath his chin.

I'm gonna count to ten. And then I want to see how fast you two can run.

CHAPTER 3

Nostalgia was thick on Morning Glory Lane. When Natalie and Teddy were kids, Bernier's back roads were their playground, the perfect hiding place. Or so it had seemed. The abandoned house on the hill had always been their turning-back point, the sign that they'd strayed too far from home.

Natalie found her cousin sitting on his bike, one foot on the ground, one on the pedal, posed like a sandpiper as he stared up at the house. His shoulder blades were sharp against his polo shirt, hair stirred around his collar by the breeze.

She braked beside Teddy. He looked over and said, "Man, you stink."

"You're loving this, aren't you?"

"*Pssh*. Try being kitchen bitch at your mom's beck and call." He grinned. "That fish-and-fried-food cologne gets old real fast. Any cats follow you here?"

Natalie rubbed her thumb and forefinger together. "World's tiniest violin."

"Don't even. You know she had to fill out some special paper to make it legal to work me to death last summer, before I turned fifteen?" He sighed. "You know why your dad never wanted to run the Grill? Because Grampie made him work out back, too, when he was my age. PTSD."

Teddy's preppy outfit was rumpled, straight from the hamper. He didn't care about clothes and wore whatever Cilla bought him, khakis and Izod shirts, the sensible old-dude sneakers nobody else their age would' be caught dead in. It put a target on his back, but one had always been there; Teddy was exactly who he was, no filter. Somebody who got excited over rare lunar events, and collecting butterflies, and World War II specials on public TV.

Her smile faded. She looked off toward the house. "I ran into Lowell Emerick today."

Teddy was quiet a moment. "They're all still around, you know. Lowell, Jason, Grace."

"Cilla talked with my folks about it. They almost didn't let me stay with you guys because of them. Like it all happened yesterday." She shook her head. "Craziness."

"So you're saying you're okay with everything? You're over it. I have to go to school with those guys—well, not Jason, he dropped out—and I'm not over it. Not even close."

"I'm not over anything. But I'm not going to let it rule our whole summer. We've got way more important stuff to worry about. Like, this house? Like the dream."

Teddy cleared his throat and glanced away. "Right. Message received, zero distortion."

"Good." She straightened her shoulders. "The dream changed last night. The door I told you about, with the glass panes in the top? This time, there were voices behind it, calling my name. I think the house knows I'm reaching out. I mean"—she looked at the house, backlit by the afternoon sun—"something's pulling me to this place. Like, I can *feel* it. Standing this close, I can feel it even stronger." She put a hand to her chest. "Right here. Whenever I wake up from the dream, there it is. Like I belong here or something."

"You belong in a rat-infested death trap. Good theory." He followed her into the weeds and up the path they'd made yesterday. "Unless . . ."

She rolled her eyes. "Go on. Impress me, genius boy."

"Unless it really *is* just a recurring dream, and all the stuff in it—the snow, the dishes, and now the voices—are only brain farts. You know, symbols or whatever. You said the dream started after you moved away from Bernier. So, maybe it had a lot to do with what happened before you left—all the stress and everything." He threw his hands up, ready to duck and cover. "Just saying."

She pondered this, and then shook her head. "No. I know the inside of that house, and it knows me. We're connected."

"Uh-huh. Are we quoting *Ghost Hunters* now?"

"I figured it out myself, thanks. But shows like that aren't that far off. I've read all about it, okay? Making electronic voice phenomena recordings is something that lots of paranormal investigators do. You don't have to use high-tech equipment to capture something, either. One of the earliest documented EVPs was made in Germany by a guy recording bird calls on a Victrola. When he played the record back, his dead wife spoke to him from the white noise."

"You know what?" Teddy stopped. "This is nuts."

"No kidding."

"No, Nat." When she turned back, Teddy's expression was uncertain. "Maybe we should leave the recorder up there. I'll buy you another one, okay? Let's forget this."

She looked at him, then at the house. Late-afternoon shadows stretched long. "I'll grab it and come right back down."

He checked his phone. "T minus three minutes and counting."

She went through the back door into the kitchen, scooping up the recorder. Her gaze was drawn to the wall—just a wall, nothing more—where the door to January stood in her dream. Gingerly, she rapped on it, waiting for an echo, some sign of a hidden room or passageway. Solid.

When they got back to Aunt Cilla's, they headed for the summerhouse, where Natalie would be staying for the next couple of months. Teddy's father Michael Finley, who'd been killed in a car crash when Teddy was three, had built the summerhouse himself. Carpentry was Michael's hobby; he'd also carved a bird hotel and mounted it outside on a post, where Natalie and Teddy used to leave secret messages for each other when they were little.

The summerhouse had one room. Natalie had moved in a bureau and a cot from the house, stacking the most vital of her collection of parapsychology and ghost-hunting books by the head of her bed. Now, she and Teddy sat on the mattress with the recorder between them. She pressed PLAY.

First, her own voice spoke: "This is Natalie Rose Payson . .

."—static—"If somebody here is"—*hhhsssshh* . . . her tone dipped—"trying to reach"—and the rest of the message faded into static.

The tape hissed on and on. A steady pounding ran beneath the white noise, like a heartbeat. Natalie and Teddy stared at each other. Then, out of nowhere:

"Tell me my regiment."

Natalie gasped.

It was a man's deep voice, trembling, as if the recording was very old, degraded.

"Do it."

"Thirteenth Army Infantry." A girl's voice, small and strange. "You walked point."

"And tell me your name." He waited. "I want to hear you say it."

The girl gave a keening whine. Static surged in. Through it cut a hoarse wail that made Natalie raise her hands to her ears.

Scrabbling, like claws against wood. Then *pound-pound-pound* again, endlessly.

The sounds stopped.

After a long pause, Teddy said softly, "What . . . the hell was that?"

It took Natalie a while to find her voice. "I have no idea."

Dad answered on the second ring.

"Kiddo, how you doing?" Over his shoulder: "I got Nat on the line."

Natalie pictured Mom sitting in the recliner with her knitting, putting her feet up after a long day cleaning rooms at the Spruce

Lodge, the only motel in Lincoln.

"So, how'd your first day at the Grill go?" Dad said. "Knock 'em dead?"

"Vice versa. I suck."

"Ah, give it two weeks. You'll be running circles around the best of them. How's that cousin of yours? Behavin'?"

"Never."

Natalie held the handset of Cilla's old house phone to her ear, looking at the photos of Teddy decorating Cilla's living room. Teddy, receiving gold cups in science fairs and physics competitions, certificates of academic excellence. He was shorter than the other winners, standing apart. Teddy had always been an honor roll student, but after Natalie moved away, he'd developed a drive that was a little scary; at fifteen, he already owned a shelf full of SAT prep books and knew exactly what universities he was going to apply to, MIT being number one on the list.

"Bernier been treating you right?" What Dad meant was, has anyone messed with you yet.

"Dad. I can handle it. Seriously."

Mom picked up the bedroom extension. "Are you really sleeping in that mildewy old summerhouse? Even though Cilla has a perfectly good guest room?"

"I like it out there. I cleaned it up. It's actually pretty nice now."

"Whatever you say. Don't let the blackflies carry you off in your sleep." Mom paused. "Miss you around here, baby. Maybe sending you down there wasn't the best idea."

This time, Natalie made herself take a deep breath before she answered. Saying she was sixteen, not six, wouldn't help her case.

"No way. I can make great tips. Everybody back home's busy this summer, anyway. Kacey and Sam are working in Bar Harbor, Mai's in summer school . . ."

Dad made a sound in his throat. "Put my sister on."

Cilla was fixing a cup of tea in the kitchen, and she carried it with her when she took the phone. "Oh, sure. Stick me in the hot seat," she said. Clearing her throat, she said into the receiver, "Hi, Billy. How's everything?"

Natalie ran upstairs and knocked on Teddy's bedroom door. He was hunched over his desk, working on a B-19 bomber. He didn't look up as she sat on the bed. Model building was Teddy's passion, along with those horrible thousand-piece jigsaw puzzles that made her eyes cross. Planes hung from the ceiling by strands of fishing line, and tanks and cars cluttered the shelves.

She took the recorder from her pocket and held it in her lap, fidgeting.

"Will you listen to it again with me?" Her voice was soft.

"No."

"But we caught something. I mean, do you know what this—" She stopped herself, took a deep breath. "I understand if you're scared, okay? So am I. But . . ."

Teddy set his paintbrush down with a click. "I am not. Scared."

His gaze was hot, indignant. Natalie looked at the floor for a moment. She should've known better than to go there with him.

He pushed back from the table, screwing the tops back on his bottles of paint.

"It's not real. It's a fake, a joke—don't you know that? That house sat wide open after we left yesterday. Obviously, somebody was either in the house listening to us when we left the recorder, or came in later and decided to mess with our heads."

She watched him. This was Teddy with his back against the wall, digging in. She ran her fingers over the silver case of the recorder. "Will you go back there with me?"

He exhaled through his nose. "I'd never ditch you. Just don't expect me to believe we're listening to ghosts."

That night, as Natalie slept, the three lights emerged from her and danced again. For a time, they clustered at the window, gazing out at the moonlit backyard, whispering together, their energy making faint pinging sounds off the wire-mesh screen.

CHAPTER 4

The jukebox sat in the back of the Grill, glowing mellow shades of cherry, lemon, and lime. Lately, it had been eating people's quarters.

Lowell Emerick arrived carrying a toolbox. His gaze was sharp; his grin was slow. His features hinted at Penobscot Indian Heritage, and he had a languid way of moving, his arms sinewy and browned from outdoor work.

Natalie stood behind the counter, learning the finer points of the soft-serve machine from Delia, but she turned to watch him walk the length of the dining room. He didn't look back until he reached the jukebox, and then only for a moment, some of the sardonic humor fading from his expression. Her body responded by tensing like a fist. She was suddenly aware of everything about herself: her long awkward legs, not exactly fat but nowhere near skinny, her zillions of freckles, the way her Payson's Grill T-shirt hugged too tightly across her chest and shoulders.

"You're overflowing, girl. Hey." Delia shoved the lever up.

"What's he doing here?"

"Him? Doing his MacGyver thing. Why?"

Teddy emerged from the kitchen, wearing an apron and carrying a tub for dirty dishes. He tended to keep his head down at work and say little; you might find him peeling potatoes with a paperback propped open in front of him or scrubbing dishes with the kitchen radio tuned to NPR. Teddy stopped abruptly at the sight of Lowell removing the juke's back panel.

Natalie said, "Did you know about this?"

A muscle moved in his jaw. "No."

Cilla had waitressed through the breakfast rush and now stood talking with a couple of the regulars. Natalie wanted to pull her away, but Delia held up the oozing sundae dish.

"The thing about ice cream is . . ."

"Oh. Sorry."

Natalie had thought her biggest challenge today would be not grabbing Teddy to rehash the tape again. She'd hardly slept, and the idea of breakfast made her stomach dry up like a pork rind; all she could think about was going to the house again. Now there was Lowell Emerick to think about.

As Delia passed the Wurlitzer, she nudged him with her toe. "I want that thing running by noon, mister, or it's your ass."

"Yes, ma'am." His voice was wry, lower than Natalie remembered.

"I got my eye on you."

The corner of his mouth turned up. "Oh, I know."

Delia had a little more swish in her walk after that.

Stiffly, Natalie checked on her tables—she'd forgotten to bring somebody a refill and the lady at table three had said *no* bacon, please—when she noticed the girls at the last booth, whispering. They were about her age, and vaguely familiar. Probably seventh graders when she was in eighth grade at Bernier Middle School.

They saw her looking, put their heads together, glanced at Lowell, and then back at her.

Heat flooded Natalie's cheeks. As she walked back to the counter to grab the decaf pot, she snuck a look at Lowell. He was staring right at her, one of his brows slightly raised, as if she'd caught him unawares. He jabbed a screwdriver into the juke's guts. At once, Natalie was livid.

Cilla was still chatting away, but Natalie cut in. "Can we talk in the office?"

Teddy stopped in the middle of clearing a table and followed.

"Did you ask Lowell to come here today?" Natalie said, crossing her arms. When Cilla nodded: "What for?"

"Because I knew he could fix the juke. He's got a knack."

Teddy snorted.

Cilla's lips thinned. Her hair was twisted up high on her head, and three pencils stuck out of her bun, forgotten. "He fixed the ice machine and replaced one of the ranges, didn't he?"

"Yeah. And I still don't understand why we have to be the ones to throw him a bone whenever he needs work." Two spots of color had appeared on Teddy's cheekbones.

Natalie flopped her arms down helplessly, glancing back toward the dining room. "Everybody's looking at us. Talking about us."

Cilla squeezed her shoulder. "Hon, I'm sorry. You're gonna have to let them talk."

Five minutes later, Lowell deposited a quarter in the juke. Music jolted from the speakers and the dining room broke into applause. Not seeming embarrassed in the slightest, he tipped his hat and stooped to gather his tools.

Natalie gave two customers refills on their coffee, watching over their heads as Cilla said to Lowell, "So, what was wrong with it?"

"Not sure." Lowell wiped his hands on a rag. "I cleaned some old grease off the amp chassis, replaced a couple wires in the control box. Did the trick."

As Cilla slipped him some bills from the cash register, the entrance bells jingled and a slim, hard-bodied girl with short tawny hair spilling over her brow and a tattoo on her arm leaned into the Grill. The last time Natalie saw Grace Thibodeau, she'd worn her hair in a single wild braid.

Grace looked at Lowell. "You set?" He nodded. "Then let's go."

Through the plate-glass window, Natalie watched them cross the parking lot and climb into a big white pickup idling at the curb. The driver was a silhouette. As they took off down Main Street, Natalie muttered, "Glad to see nothing's changed," and slapped a dishrag down on the counter. Delia looked at her curiously.

Teddy found a broken board in the weeds outside the house on Morning Glory Lane and gave it a practice swing.

Natalie watched him. "Ready to bust some ectoplasmic heads?"

"I'm not checking this place out without a weapon." He squinted at the upstairs windows. "Some wackadoo on crank could be squatting upstairs, waiting for those stupid kids to come back again."

"Or maybe we experienced something real. Do you know how special that would be? I mean, we made a genuine EVP recording. Contact with the other side. Hardly anybody in the world can say that."

"The other side can stay right where it is. I'm good." But she was already walking toward the barn. He ran to catch up.

The barn roof had collapsed, bowing the structure, forcing the double doors open wide enough that Natalie could slide through. She jerked back just as quickly, heart pounding: The haymow floor was rotted straight through, revealing a gaping blackness into the foundation. Overhead, a sparrow fluttered across the patch of blue sky exposed in the rafters.

"Forget it," she said, and they went into the house.

Natalie scuffed her sneaker over the dusty floor.

"See? The only footprints are ours." She sighed; the house was stillness itself compared to the Grill. "You know, I'm starting to understand what it was like for you. Staying in Bernier, letting everybody talk. You said last night that you'd never ditch me. But I ditched you."

"You didn't ditch me. Your dad took that job in Lincoln. It was good for you guys." He walked ahead of her, making samurai sword *shing!* sound effects as he swatted cobwebs. "It wasn't so bad. I mean, it *was*. But after seventh grade, everybody pretty much forgot about Peter and gossiped about other junk." He was quiet. "It was kind of gross, actually."

Natalie said nothing. It occurred to her that she'd probably been gossiping about the same junk at Lincoln Academy—who was crushing on who, who was flunking, whatever—acting like she was normal, like she'd never had a gun cocked in her face, never run through these woods waiting for a bullet to slam through her back. Normal. Except for the nightmare, of course; her secret reminder that she was anything but.

The first night she'd spent in their new house in Lincoln, she'd had the dream, and it had persisted ever since; not every night, but at least twice a week, waking with a pounding heart and an inescapable feeling that she'd left something behind in Bernier. Something that badly wanted her to return. She'd told no one but Teddy, and even then only in e-mails, giving her a little distance from what was happening to her. As far as she could see, it either meant she was crazy, or haunted. Neither one was a good opener when trying to make new friends.

Together, they checked out the first floor. Kitchen, dining room, two parlors, a bathroom with a sludgy toilet. Upstairs, the bedrooms were empty, mildewed. One doorway contained a narrow staircase, and they stopped together at the foot.

"Ugh," Teddy whispered. The air in the forgotten attic was redolent with scat and decay, as close as a hand pressed over your mouth.

A headache began pulsing at Natalie's temples. "Let's not." She shut the door. They went back downstairs, leaving the attic to its slumber.

"I call the left-hand parlor for recording number two. We'll see what happens."

Natalie stopped in front of the soot-smeared hearth and set the recorder on the mantel, pressing the button.

"*Frank-ie and John-ny were lov-errrs—love-errrrrsloverrrs—*"

They both jumped. The RECORD button was depressed, yet a voice was coming from the speaker, a girl's monotonous singing echoing through the room.

"*O Lordy, how they could looove . . .*"

There came the sound of the girl's light footsteps, as if she were crossing the parlor. They seemed to pass right by Natalie and Teddy, heading out to the foyer.

There was a screen-door creak.

"Good morning." It was her, the same girl who'd said *Thirteenth Army Infantry* on the last recording.

"Morning, miss—got your milk delivery," said a man with a thick Maine accent. "Gorry, hope I didn't wake you." He sounded like the old duffers who came into the Grill to swap stories.

"I wake up with the birds." She said it proudly, like a child, interrupted by heavy glass bottles clinking together. "Do you want to see what I can do?"

Whatever it was, it was lost in a wave of static that rose and receded. Then they were saying their good-byes, the milkman chuckling, the door creaking shut again.

White silence.

Heavy footsteps. Natalie felt goose bumps break out over her body like a rash.

A man spoke—*the* man, from the first recording—his voice deep and slow. "You just don't want to learn." He said something else in a harsh foreign dialect.

The girl ran. He chased. Their footsteps seemed to pound off down the hallway.

Natalie grabbed the recorder and followed, holding the recorder out like a divining rod; she was closing space between them, the footsteps growing louder on the tape.

The footsteps went into the kitchen, where there was a crash that made Natalie cry out, like a piece of furniture being shoved aside. Natalie, with Teddy on her heels, cleared the kitchen threshold in time to hear a door—later, they both agreed they'd felt a gust of cold air—slam in the far wall.

It was the same wall where the door to January stood in Natalie's dream.

CHAPTER 5

"You two sure are putting a lot of mileage on those bikes." Cilla watched them from across the table.

Supper was chipped beef on toast, aka, paste on cardboard; Natalie couldn't taste a thing. She felt as if she were soaring inside, weightless, unable to settle into her own body.

"I almost never ride in Lincoln." Natalie forced down another bite, shooting Teddy a look. He hadn't touched his meal. He was too busy staring into space, looking pale and stricken, practically advertising that something was wrong. "Too many pulp trucks. I can't wait until I get my own car."

Cilla chewed slowly. "Mind if I ask where you've been going lately?"

"All over," Natalie said at the same time Teddy said, "Around." Cilla stared at them. "Mm-hmm."

They finished the meal in silence, but when Cilla pushed her chair back, she said, "Nat, give me a hand with the dishes?"

Teddy hung around while the sink filled, brushing at crumbs on the counter and stalling. Cilla finally said, "For God's sake, go find something to do. I'm not going to bite her."

"All *right*, I'm going." He stood holding the screen door open until Cilla spun on him, and then he stomped down the steps into the yard.

Cilla plunged her hands into the suds. "I wanted to say thanks for hanging in there at work today. It's not going to be easy, but you won't be such a novelty forever. People will quit gawking." She shook her head. "Small towns have long memories."

"I guess."

"Have you been down to see your folks' old house?"

"No."

"Nice family living there."

The subject of Lowell Emerick swelled between them until Natalie couldn't take it anymore.

"So what's Lowell's deal? He's like Bernier's lovable Mr. Fix-it now?"

"On the side." Cilla's tone was mild. "He's working for LaBrie Landscaping this summer, too."

"He must like money."

"He needs it. He helps his dad pay the bills. Fred isn't really up to holding a steady job anymore." Cilla made a *glug-glug* gesture.

"Shocker."

"Lowell was never the worst of them, Natalie."

"No, that was Jason, followed by Grace. And it looks like the threesome's still tight. Too bad Peter isn't around anymore. They could keep smoking weed under the train trestle and setting off cherry bombs forever."

Cilla stopped scrubbing. Shame flooded in, and Natalie shut her eyes.

"I didn't mean it. About Peter."

Cilla nodded, taking her time rinsing. "Nat . . . try to remember.

Just because something looks a certain way doesn't mean that's how it is. It's been two years. People can change a lot." She gave her a sidelong glance. "Especially when they're young."

Later, Natalie went outside in search of Teddy. An early moon hung in a sky of lapis. She found him at the badminton net, bouncing a shuttlecock. She picked up the other racket. "Serve."

He did, and they played a while. When their gazes finally met, it was as if they still stood together in the nightmare house, in that cacophony of sound. The shuttlecock landed in the grass.

"What do you want to do now?" He sounded hoarse.

"Keep going back. Find out about the house, who lived there."

She was amazed to find that she'd already made her decision, even though she could still feel the goose bumps on her skin.

"I think I have to. You don't." She held her breath, waiting.

Finally, Teddy shook his head. "Uh-uh. I'm sticking with you."

In the dream kitchen, flurries drifted. Natalie opened the door with six panes of glass. Frigid air swirled out, stirring her hair.

The girls' voices whispered around her, calling her name.

"Hello?" Natalie said, gripping the door frame. There was a sensation of being pulled forward, of losing gravity. She felt herself leave the threshold, passing through the door for the first time.

She drifted into the blackness. Snow pelted through the void, generating its own cold light. "Who are you? How do you know my name?" she asked.

They answered at once, a hissing legion.
"We are the weavers. We are the shearers."
Silence.
"And you are the darning needle."
Their laughter followed, melodic, inhuman, like the ringing of
silver chimes.

Natalie awoke to light, and the conviction that she wasn't alone in the room.

She opened her eyes, blinking against a burned afterimage on her lids, much like the imprint left by staring too long into the sun. Yet the summerhouse was dark. Her alarm clock read 3:32 a.m.

For a long time, she huddled under the sheets. The dream burned inside her.

Eventually, she became aware of the sound of something moving around outside. The summerhouse backed on the woods, and as Natalie listened, she heard dead leaves crunching underfoot. Not a raccoon, not a deer. Heavier.

A bulb with a pull chain hung from the rafters, and Natalie turned it on, going to the door and stepping outside in her pajamas and bare feet.

She waited. It only occurred to her later to feel fear. She felt cloaked in the dream, not fully in this world and therefore in no danger. She wanted to see who was out there.

For the longest time, there was silence. Perhaps the visitor had heard her. Perhaps there was no one there at all. Natalie shut the door, got back under the covers.

Only once she had nearly surrendered to sleep again did she think she heard footsteps moving off into the night.

CHAPTER 6

The next morning, she awoke to a knock on the door. Teddy stood outside on the step, holding a backpack. "Provisions. We'll need them later."

"Later? Are we having a picnic?"

"We'll probably have to work through lunch." When she blinked, he snapped his fingers under her nose. "Finding out the history of the house—who used to live there? Any of that sound familiar?"

"Quit it." She swatted his hand away. As she turned, she noticed that the bird hotel's miniature door was open. It was their old signal, hers and Teddy's, when one of them had left a message for the other.

"Did you . . .?" When Teddy shook his head, Natalie went to the house and lifted the roof.

The object inside was simultaneously familiar and strange. Natalie turned it over in her fingers, thinking of footsteps in the dark. "Something happened last night."

As she told him about it, Teddy took the barrette from her hand. Familiar, yes, because every little girl on the planet had probably worn something like it once: molded white plastic with a metal clasp.

"It's not yours?" he said.

"When was the last time you saw me wear barrettes?" She bit her thumbnail. "Who else could've known how we used the bird hotel, anyway? Other than our parents. Maybe it was in there this whole time."

Teddy pushed the small door shut with his finger. "Birds sure left in a hurry."

The Historical Society donation box had a sign asking for $1.00 minimum. A tiny woman with a white bouffant hairdo sat behind the desk reading a paperback.

"Hel-lo, wel-come," she sang out as Natalie and Teddy came in.

Natalie searched her pockets. She had seventy-six cents. She nudged Teddy. He scrounged up a dime and dropped their change through the slot.

"Sorry," he said, turning red.

"Short, are we?" the woman said. "That's all right. So am I. Buh-bum-ching. I don't suppose you're interested in the tour. People rarely are." She studied them with small, bright eyes. "Unless you're the rare sort? Do you thrill to the sight of antique quilts and china sets?"

Natalie laughed. "Not really. We're looking for some information about an old house out on Morning Glory Lane. Who owned it and when they lived there. The clerk over at the Town Office said you guys have a collection of papers on that stuff?"

"Oh, yes. A gift from a local historian. Don't tell me you two vibrant young people want to spend your summer afternoon tracing property titles?" They nodded, and she got to her feet. "Splendid. I knew you were the rare sort the moment I laid eyes on you."

Fans gossiped overhead as Natalie and Teddy bent over a grantee book, tall as an atlas and pungent with dust. *25 Morning Glory Lane*. Natalie ran her fingertip beneath the text.

"Somebody owns it. Howard and Catherine Foster. Bought the place in 1998."

"They left it to fall apart like that?" Teddy said, shoving his glasses up the bridge of his nose. "Maybe they were driven out, like, *Amityville*-style. Maybe you're not the only one the ghosts have talked to."

Natalie folded her arms on the table. "I am, though."

"You're just that special?"

How could you explain a gut conviction?

"The tape recordings aren't from 1998, anyway. A milkman? Really?" She flipped to the house's first ownership. "Built in 1772 by Captain Nathaniel Leary. Originally sat on one hundred and thirty acres of land. There's a note that the barn and some outbuildings were added in 1820. They turned it into a farm." She flipped through the next few pages. "The Leary family owned it for over a hundred and fifty years. Then it was bought by a guy named George Dawes in 1947. He sold it in 1949. The next owner, Harriet Forsythe, held on to it until 1970. Empty again until the Fosters."

Natalie dropped back in her chair. "None of those names sound foreign. I was kind of hoping it'd be obvious who we were listening to. I mean, I don't even know what language that man was speaking—"

"Russian. I think."

"Well. You little Rosetta Stone, you."

"I think you need to expand your cultural education beyond *Syfy*, Nat."

"Ha." Natalie thought. "What if we're listening to some time period not long after World War Two? Our deep-talking guy served in the Thirteenth Army Infantry, and the song the girl sang sounded like big-band music, didn't it? And getting a milk delivery would've been weird if the house was still a farm."

"George Dawes," Teddy said. "It must be him."

Excitement played cat's cradle with her insides. "You're into war stuff. Did American soldiers ever need to learn Russian during World War Two?"

"Maybe. Russia allied with Great Britain after Germany invaded their country, so we were all sort of on the same side."

"Huh. Well, whoever George Dawes was, he didn't stay in Bernier long." She rubbed her arms. "They say that some ghosts are imprints, like memories of tragedy stamped on a place, replaying over and over again. Those tapes make me feel sick, and the nightmare is getting weirder. Do you think I could be picking up on psychic fallout left behind by George Dawes and that girl?"

Teddy thought for a moment. "Psychic fallout? Maybe. The thing I don't get is, why you?"

Inside 25 Morning Glory Lane, Natalie and Teddy sat in the left-hand parlor with the recorder between them. Natalie pressed the button.

Nothing.

Why should they be allowed to pick up where they left off? The house wanted to wind them up, watch them bump into walls before teetering off in a new direction.

"Another room, then," Natalie said. "Maybe it wants us to explore."

Teddy cleared his throat. "Yay."

They selected a small bedroom upstairs. When they pressed RECORD, the sound of an old-fashioned sewing machine came from the speaker, *thud-thud-thud*, and then a pause as the operator adjusted the fabric before working the foot pedal again. In another bedroom, silence. In the next, weeping. It was muffled, as if the person was sobbing hard into their bent arm or a pillow. Natalie's own body felt wracked with it.

"Sounds like a man," Teddy said softly. "Doesn't it?"

Goose bumps tickled up her legs. "Okay. That's enough for today."

They were almost to the back door when she changed her mind.

She went into the kitchen, to the wall with the invisible door. She held out the recorder.

Hhsshh. This time it wasn't static coming from the speaker. It was wind, whispering around a door left ajar.

Natalie followed the invisible seam, running her fingers over the wall.

"Pen?" she said.

Teddy dug in the backpack until he produced one. She traced

the doorframe on the wall in blue ink, had nearly finished when there was a *click* from the speaker. The wind stopped.

Someone, somewhere, had closed the door.

Heebie-jeebies drove them all the way down the hill to their bikes, where they stopped to catch their breath. They'd forgotten to eat the lunch Teddy had packed, so they did so as they perched on their bikes, staring up at the house.

Natalie said, "In my dream, the girls say I'm their darning needle. What do you think that means?"

Teddy chewed, thinking. "Dream code. Could be anything."

When they left, it was never their habit to look back. The glare of the windowpanes followed them. The glass was now covered in frost.

CHAPTER 7

"Heads up." Delia dodged Natalie with a platter, raising her voice above the Friday-night din. "Help me, huh?"

Natalie carried the second platter for Delia's party of eight. She'd been lost in thoughts of snow and dream riddles, but now she spied him, coming through the Grill door in a herd of customers.

Lowell. Again.

The sight of him made Natalie's stomach drop, and it finally hit her that he was exactly the kind of guy she and her girlfriends would've lusted over back home—*him*, Lowell Emerick. He was *sexy*. The same boy who used to shoot spitballs at her in the hallway and once helped Jason trip Teddy down a flight of cement steps in front of Bernier Middle.

She must've sucked in her breath. Delia glanced back. "Burn yourself?"

"Yeah." Natalie passed out crabmeat rolls and bowls of steamed clams. The crowd who'd come through the door split off into separate parties, and Natalie recognized two more faces. Jason Morrow and Grace Thibodeau. They headed toward the corner booth with some other friends, but Lowell went to the counter alone. Jason and the rest hollered and catcalled at him until he finally slid off the stool and joined them.

Delia noticed her gaze skewering the corner booth and frowned.

"Go take a breather, okay? It's almost time for your fifteen anyway. I'll find you, and then you're going to tell me what this"—she pointed between Natalie and Lowell—"is all about."

In the kitchen, Teddy was unloading dirty dishes into the sink, his hair sticking to his damp brow. "Having fun?" he said as Natalie came up beside him. "Welcome to Friday nights until Labor Day."

"Did you see who's out there?"

The corner booth was framed in the pickup window, and Teddy peered out.

Grace lolled on Jason's lap, her short hair held back by a red bandanna. Jason Morrow had changed little: He had the blunt looks of a jock, closely buzzed blond hair and a clean shave; his tattered jeans and corded necklace looked like a costume he'd ripped off some hapless metalhead. Three other kids had wedged into the booth with them, and though none of them could legally order anything stronger than Coke in the Grill, they'd obviously fueled up ahead of time.

Teddy swallowed and shoved his hair out of his face. "That's Bess's table. She'll take care of them."

The older waitress stepped up to the booth, one hand parked on her hip.

"Don't even go back there, okay?"

"What's going on?" Delia leaned in between them, bringing a whiff of sandalwood oil.

Teddy flushed and moved back.

Natalie said, "They hate us, we hate them. That about sums

41

it up." She watched her cousin remove his glasses, polishing away an invisible smudge. "Jason, Lowell, and Grace treated us like crap when we were in middle school together. The end."

"Obviously not. Every time you see Lowell, you grow claws."

Teddy made himself scarce without a word to either of them, the back of his neck still red.

Delia crossed her arms, studying Natalie. "You really want to hold a grudge this long?"

"It's not up to me." Then she went out to check on her tables.

The corner booth grew rowdy fast. Grace Thibodeau had never been a lap-sitting kind of girl when sober, but now her throaty laughter carried, and Cilla, who was running the register, finally stopped ignoring them and stared, her gaze flinty.

When Natalie locked eyes with Jason for a second, then deliberately turned her back on him, all pretenses were dropped.

Jason knocked a basket of fries onto the floor with a flick of his hand. Ketchup splattered and there was a chorus of *ohhhh*'s from the booth. Bess huffed and squatted to pick up the mess. Natalie knew she should help—Cilla and most of the Grill were watching—so she knelt down, close enough to Lowell's protruding leg to count the loose threads on the cuffs of his jeans. As she scooped up fries, she half-expected Jason's Nike to catch her under the chin; by the time she stood up, her whole body was tensed for a blow.

"Hey, there, sunshine." Jason's voice held the same false brightness it always had. The expression in his deep-set blue eyes was flat. "You're back."

Grace hiccuped over a giggle and fell silent. Lowell pushed his hat up his brow, studying the Formica table as if it held some secret code.

Natalie turned away from Jason again, simply saying "Uh-huh," as an afterthought.

"We missed you," Jason called as she walked away.

In the employee bathroom, Natalie threw water on her face, covered her eyes, and waited for her heart to stop hammering. She was not shaking. She was fine. She could handle this, any of them, all of them.

Ten minutes later, Jason's crowd got up to leave. Natalie was wiping down the counter, and Jason started swaggering over. Lowell got in his way. They had a hushed disagreement, ending with Lowell stepping back, hands held up, his expression saying, *What's it gonna be?*

Jason said, "Whatever, man. I'm gone."

Grace followed him out.

Lowell stayed. He sat at the end of the counter and ordered a coffee from Delia.

She brought it to him and rapped him on the forehead with her pen. "That's for fixing the damn juke."

He rubbed the sore spot. "Problem?"

"Only if you consider country music a problem. Hint: I do." Behind them, another tune twanged to life. Delia growled. "This is cruel and unusual."

"So file a grievance."

Delia flipped him off behind a menu and went to take an order.

Teddy, somber-faced, idled by the kitchen doors, never taking his eyes off Natalie.

Lowell took a long drink of coffee, set the cup in the saucer, and said to Natalie, "Got any cream?"

She brought it over. When she turned to leave, he reached out to stop her.

"Don't," she said, before they even touched.

He stopped. "I'm sorry."

She said nothing, her shoulders held taut.

"I don't want to . . . I didn't come in here to hassle you."

"No, you came in here to back up your buddy." She forced herself to look him in the eye. His hazel eyes were clear, nearly blue in this light. "Don't you ever get tired of following Jason around?"

That hit a tender spot. It was satisfying to see the air of humor, which seemed to keep him buoyant, disappear for once. He braced his hands against the edge of the counter. "Hear me out. Two seconds."

"I don't have two seconds for you." She turned, working the rag over the back counter until she heard the bells over the door jingle. He was gone.

CHAPTER 8

It rained the next day. Natalie and Teddy got off work at two o'clock and rode their bikes to 25 Morning Glory Lane, which looked as dark and crumpled as wet cardboard.

"What did he think he could say?" Natalie went on. They'd been having this conversation in fits and starts since they'd left the Grill. "There's nothing *to* say."

"Maybe something like, 'Oops, sorry I used to torture you guys, but if you could let me off the hook now, that'd be awesome.' " Teddy was quiet a second. "None of them have tried to talk to me. Ever."

"Yeah, well. Lucky you."

"It's Peter's family they should apologize to, anyway." They continued up the hill, lost in thought, and then Teddy shook himself. "Lowell's weird. Mom says he keeps himself to himself."

"Really? He seems pretty out there to me. I guess that's his role, right? Jason's the douchebag leader, Lowell's the smartass sidekick, Grace is . . . I dunno. Gangster's girlfriend."

Teddy gave a thin smile. "I guess Mom thinks Lowell's got this heart of gold underneath it all."

Natalie snorted. "Whatever he's got, Delia sure seems to like it."

Teddy kept his gaze down, tugging the drawstrings of his windbreaker. "All waitresses have to flirt to make tips." He accepted her punch in the arm. They'd reached the back door of the house. "No more footsteps outside last night, right?" he said, scrutinizing her. "Nothing new in the bird hotel?"

"I would've told you."

Natalie gasped when she stepped inside. It was freezing in the corridor. A chill breeze wafted in and out of the rooms, twining around her bare legs. Without sunshine, it was dark enough to need a flashlight—Teddy had packed one, ever the Boy Scout (he'd made Eagle Scout last fall)—and they walked to the foyer with the beam lighting their way.

"What is this?" she asked.

Teddy watched his breath plume in the air, then shone the beam on the sidelights flanking the front door. "Look." He leaned into the parlor, shining the light around. "All the windows are frosted over. In June."

Gooseflesh rose on Natalie's skin. "We'd better get started." She pulled out the recorder and pressed the button.

Pound-pound-pound-pound. The thudding from the first recording was back, impossibly loud, thundering from the speaker until Natalie threw the recorder down with a cry. It skidded across the floorboards and chirped into silence.

"Nat!"

Teddy's voice was distant. She turned, feeling leaden. He was reaching out to her, but time was dallying around them, spinning out like a top, everything moving in slow motion.

She stumbled and fell to her knees. There was light now, blue and strange, coming from her. Sparking, building, encasing her hands as she held them up before her face, disbelieving. She looked at Teddy, thinking *How can he still be so far away?*

With that, Natalie Payson ceased to be.

SPRING 1948

Rachel chased the kitten beneath the wood cookstove, where it mewed, crouching among ashes and shadows.

Rachel reached for it, and Mrs. Page placed her foot lightly on her arm. "If you want to burn your hand off, keep right on doing what you're doing."

Rachel stood. Her long dark hair was braided and pinned in a crown on her head, and she wore a baggy housedress with a full apron and no shoes. The girl's eyes were wide, black, inscrutable. A simpleton, poor little devil. How old could she be—eighteen? Nineteen?

"Don't tell. Please-please."

"All I want you to do is help me with this cake. I won't say boo to your brother if you'll just be still. These cooking lessons are for your own good."

Together, they turned the cake out onto a cooling rack. Mrs. Page had met the girl at church; their farm was just down the road, and George's sister seemed sharp enough to learn her way around a kitchen. With George's shy ways, he'd never ask for help teaching her. He kept out of the big house entirely while Mrs. Page was there, the sound of hammering from the workshop the only proof he was home at all.

She noticed a doll in Rachel's apron pocket. "Who's this, now?"

Rachel bit her lips, watching as Mrs. Page sifted powdered sugar into a bowl for frosting, then whispered, "Her name's Hazel."

"Any reason she's got no clothes on?" Mrs. Page held out a spoon. "Stir."

The girl obeyed. "She got stripped naked. All she's got is a sweater over her face." Down the hall, a clock sang a tune of varied chimes. "She's cold and she misses her mama and papa in New Ashford."

A scrap of knitting was tied over the doll's porcelain face, mussing its golden ringlets.

"Is that where you came from, too? Massachusetts?"

The Dawes family's origins were a mystery to Mrs. Page and the rest of Bernier. They were hardly the sort of people you could ask flat out. They were private.

Rachel nodded.

"You must miss it, too." Mrs. Page paused. "Do you have kin there?"

"No. We had to leave. It wasn't a place for decent folk anymore."

A door closed somewhere. A moment later, George could be seen through the window, crossing the dooryard. Mrs. Page adjusted her spectacles. He was a queer character; such a slow, awkward manner, so reluctant to meet a lady's eye. He was a great big dark fella, six and a half feet high, broad through the shoulders and chest, with a hitch in his walk from an Italian bullet during the War. He seemed to take no interest in bird-dogging the young gals, who, in Mrs. Page's estimation, could do a lot worse.

Once the cake was frosted, Mrs. Page gathered her coat and pocketbook. Rachel followed her outside, holding her hand. "You'll come back?"

" 'Course. You keep well, wild girl. Last time I stopped by, your brother told me you were feeling poorly."

George came out of the workshop then, hauling lumber, a cigarette clamped in his teeth.

"Appreciate your time. Sorry for the bother." His voice was husky and deep.

"No bother." There was a honk as Mr. Page brought his Packard to a halt at the foot of the drive. Mrs. Page smiled and smoothed Rachel's flyaway hair. "See you soon, dear. Take good care of Hazel." She winked.

The way George stared, he must've thought his sister's daftness was catching.

Once brother and sister stood alone, he grabbed her arm. He knew just how far to bend it back. Rachel shrieked. He dug into her apron pocket and pulled out the doll. In their shared language, he said, "I told you not to fool with me."

She ran. He pursued at a measured pace, tapping the ash

from his Chesterfield King.

The milk house was closest. She ran inside and pushed an old milk can under the knob so the door couldn't be opened, then sank down, hugging her knees.

The doorknob rotated. Rachel—this was not her real name—shut her eyes, looking up only when she was sure she'd waited long enough and he'd be gone.

It was nearly dark when she emerged. The yard was deserted. She'd sneak in through the back door and climb the stairs to her room. He'd probably leave her be now. On her way, she found her doll lying in the yellow spring grass. Its face had been crushed.

Natalie opened her eyes to blackness. She was curled up in a small space. Reaching out, she felt shelves, empty, gritty with dust. She pounded her fist. "Hey!"

Running footsteps approached, and then a doorway opened in the darkness. She sat up, squinting.

Teddy pulled her out of the kitchen pantry into a hug. "Where the hell have you *been?*"

She couldn't speak.

"I thought you were dead. How'd you get in there?" He shook her, almost in tears. "Tell me where you went!"

She sank to her knees. "Here. In this room. Only I wasn't me. And it wasn't now, it . . ."

She covered her face.

He squatted beside her, breathing hard. "I looked everywhere. There was light all over you, Nat. Then you were gone."

"I saw them."

"*Who?*"

"I know things they didn't even say out loud, things they were only *thinking*. I was inside their heads—"

She knew she was babbling and shut her mouth, rocking slightly. On the opposite wall, the doorframe she'd drawn in ink stood dimly defined.

CHAPTER 9

Cilla's front porch was a refuge from the rain. Natalie sat cocooned in a quilt, watching runoff drip into the rhododendron bushes along the latticework.

Teddy said again, "The neighbor lady's name was Page? There aren't any other farmhouses on Morning Glory now. Just woods."

Mrs. Page. A plump lady of sixty whose arms dimpled like uncooked bread dough and whose eyes required strong spectacles. "Maybe it was torn down. Or fell down."

He blew out a breath, resting his chin on his folded arms. "Could the whole thing have been a hallucination? You were only gone for about fifteen minutes. Maybe you didn't go anywhere except in your mind."

"But how did I get inside that pantry? I'm telling you, I *know* it was real. Some part of me was really there. What I can't figure out is why you didn't come with me." Natalie watched the rain. "Rachel Dawes was lying about her name. George, too, I guess."

"In the first recording, George asked her about her name, didn't he? Maybe she had a hard time remembering the lie."

"And don't forget the doll. He was really going to hurt her over that."

"Did you bring back any memories about him, like you did with Mrs. Page?"

"I got a feeling, all right. I don't like him."

Words weren't strong enough. George, his face remarkably handsome from one angle, and that of a prizefighter from another, repelled her completely. It was a visceral reaction, from the gut. She no longer felt so snug in her chair and stood to go inside.

Teddy said quietly, "We shouldn't go back to that house."

"Then what? What if the nightmare never stops?" Natalie shook her head, letting the screen door close on her final words, "I can't give up yet."

Natalie followed the girls' whispers through the darkness and spitting snow of the dream plane.

"Look." Their voices spoke as one. The snow swirled, solidified, made ground beneath her feet, a semblance of surroundings that grew brighter, more real.

She was on a winter road, familiar to her, surrounded by woods capped in snow.

It was flurrying here, too. There were footprints along the shoulder, heading up to the bend in the road, where a large chestnut tree stretched its branches into the gray sky. Something about those solitary footprints—boy's, size nine Converse—sent a stab of dread through her.

"Hurry, darning needle," the whispers hissed. "You know the way."

Natalie began to run.

Natalie awoke and lay there with her eyes closed. Those burned pinpoints were on the backs of her eyelids again, like faded memories of intense light.

The girls were right. She did know the way. She knew that back road. For some reason, now the dream was taking her back through the memory of that day as it had happened, the day that Jason, Lowell (damn, but it had been easier to think of him as a kid with stringy hair and zits on his chin), Grace, and Peter had cornered her and Teddy in the woods.

The day Peter McInnis had died.

Teddy had always been—well, Teddy. The kid who was such a brainiac that he'd skipped a grade, placing him in with Natalie, Jason, and the rest. Bullies lay in wait everywhere for a kid like him, but Jason's crew had taken it to the next level. Jumping Teddy downtown and really whaling on him. Slashing his bike tires. Thinking up stupid, cruel nicknames and convincing everybody in school to use them. Natalie had stuck by Teddy whenever she could, sure, but she wasn't exactly the queen of cool herself. She'd taken her share of lumps in eighth grade.

For Teddy, it had been hell.

In the spring, he'd secured a hiding place in the woods off Pemaquid Road, by a brook. He'd literally run out the school doors to Pemaquid and wait there until Natalie met up with him so they could cut home through the woods. If they were followed, they never knew.

By January, the bullies had found them. The day that Jason's crowd had stormed the woods, Jason had brought along one of his stepdad's guns. Just to scare them, he'd later claimed. Just to freak them out. But that wasn't where it had ended.

She needed air. Natalie threw the covers back and went outside, taking deep breaths.

The bird hotel door stood open again.

She looked inside. On the plywood floor lay a shell casing. Small-caliber, crimped from firing. She pulled her hand back from the bird hotel as if stung.

It wasn't *the* casing. The state police would've collected that, along with whatever other evidence had been salvageable from the forest floor that day. But it was close enough.

Natalie didn't want to touch it. She didn't want Cilla finding it, either, or Teddy. Not sure what her plan was, she forced herself to pick up the casing, then walked into the trees.

The woods were thin on Bailey Street, barely more than a screen between yards. Natalie studied the bushes and dead leaves and mud, hoping for a footprint, some obvious sign of passage. Impossible to tell.

She followed the tree line toward the street, wondering if she was taking the same path as her nighttime visitor. How could they even know she was sleeping in the summerhouse unless they'd been spying on her? Or maybe it was someone who spent a lot of time at the Grill, had overheard Cilla talking about Natalie's upcoming visit . . . someone who'd been turning up like a bad penny ever since she got here.

Certain now, Natalie reached the sidewalk and stood there, fists clenched. There was a storm drain beside the neighbor's driveway, and on impulse, she dropped the casing through the grate. It clattered once, deep down.

Back in the woods, Natalie said aloud, "I know who you are," as if he might still be watching from some secret place. Birds and insects continued their productive hum, unbothered.

CHAPTER 10

Loop Road was easy to find. All Natalie had to do was keep pedaling until Main Street became Route 15, then head up the first dirt road on the right.

The Emericks lived in a modular home surrounded by a galaxy of junk that covered the blueberry fields as far as Natalie could see: ripped-open couches, appliances, car parts. An old school bus sagged over the rise, its windows bulging with bags of trash.

Don't wuss out now. Natalie had gotten off work fifteen minutes ago, while Teddy was scheduled until nine-thirty tonight. He didn't need to know about this. She hadn't told him about the shell casing, either. None of this would be happening if she hadn't come back to Bernier. She'd stirred up a hornets' nest; now it was her job to smoke the buggers out.

Natalie picked her way up the walk and knocked on the door. Her heart was thumping so hard she was sure that the Emericks must be able to hear it inside.

Someone came up the shadowy corridor. When Lowell opened the door, she didn't fully recognize him. He wasn't wearing his ever-present Red Sox hat, and his hair looked soft, somehow making him seem younger.

His expression was hard, but there was a glint of curiosity in his eyes.

"I thought you didn't have two seconds for me."

"Do you want to talk or not?"

After a long pause, the door screeched open further.

"You're here now. Might as well come in." He made a mock-gallant sweep with his free arm.

She slid past him to prove she wasn't intimidated, her muscles knotted. It was dim inside the house. They went into a sparse living room. A television blathered.

Lowell dropped onto the couch. "So? You want me to talk, or listen?"

"I know what you're doing." She'd rehearsed these lines. "Stay off Cilla's property, and stay away from Teddy and me, or I'll tell the cops that you've been harassing us." His silence shook her. "I really will."

He stared.

"I don't expect you to own up. Just stop." Her face grew hot when he didn't speak. "You know what I'm talking about." She glanced toward the doorway, wondering who else was in the house. His drunk dad, probably, somewhere.

Lowell sighed and settled deeper into the couch, his knees spread.

"I guess you better spell it out for me, Natalie, because right now it sounds like you're talking out of your ass."

"The barrette? The shell casing. I don't know how you knew about the bird hotel thing, but it's over. This isn't junior high. You guys can't mess with us and get away with it anymore. God, haven't you grown up at all?"

He laughed. "Have you? You still think you've got me, Jason, and Grace figured, don't you? Like none of us could've changed. We're always gonna be the bad guys." He stood and smacked the power button on the TV. "I don't know what barrette you're talking about. And we don't have bullets around here. We don't keep guns in the house. Now, unless you've got some other bullshit accusations you want to throw around, there's the door. Don't let it hit ya."

Smoldering, Natalie started to go, but then she turned back.

"It has to be one of you. One of you still has the gun, right?"

It was the worst thing she could throw at him, the ugliest rumor that had circulated through Bernier's grapevine back then.

Lowell looked at her, his hands lowering to his sides.

"One of you kept it, and hid it, and left that little present for me this morning," she said. "So yeah. I'd say you're still the bad guys." She banged out of the screen door.

Natalie pedaled her bike furiously, tears blurring her vision. The next thing she knew, a horn was beeping behind her. She'd made it down to the Quik Stop in a complete haze. She swerved over to the curb and wiped her face on her sleeve.

Cilla's station wagon drew up next to her, and her aunt leaned across the seats.

"Hey, stranger. I'm on my way home. Where you headed?" Her smile faded at Natalie's expression. "What's wrong?"

"Nothing. I was going home, too." Natalie put her bike on the rack and climbed in.

They listened to the radio for a while—her aunt preferred classic country in the vein of Tammy Wynette and Loretta Lynn—until Cilla said quietly, "Do you want to tell me where you were coming from?" She waited. "Not Oak Hill, I hope." She glanced at her. "Tell me you and Teddy haven't been riding your bikes up there to Peter's grave."

"No. Why would we?" Natalie looked at her hands. She sounded like a sullen kid. "We were only friends with him when we were little. He hated us by the time he—when he died."

Cilla patted Natalie's knee gingerly. On the radio, Patsy Cline sang about walking after midnight.

CHAPTER 11

"I'm not sure I want this to happen again," Teddy said.

"It's okay. Remember to grab my hand."

"You really think you can bring me with you?"

Natalie shrugged. "I hope so. You have to see what it's like. Amazing, seriously. Like being there, only—without yourself."

She stopped at every second-story window, inspecting the frosted glass. Behind her, Teddy was jumpy, squeezing the backpack straps over his shoulders. Natalie felt an odd sensation of calm, pushing away all thoughts of yesterday's encounter with Lowell: how he'd stared back at her, his expression somehow worse than wounded, not at all the look of guilt she'd expected.

The house was what mattered now. Seeing if time would shift for her again.

Natalie crossed to the attic door in the dim morning light. The attic no longer breathed sickening heat. It was frigid now, smelling of mildew and decay.

Natalie started up the stairs.

"Wait." Teddy stood at the bottom, staring up. "Nat, look. Look at yourself!"

She looked. It had already begun.

The light came from her core, just south of her heart, building, streaking down her arms and legs, coating her body until she was nearly blind with it. She panicked, cried out, and turned to him. Their fingers linked. The final flash of light took the world away.

AUTUMN 1948

The Sawbones returned that morning, his truck stalling out in a blast of exhaust halfway up the hill. He coaxed the engine and was off again, sending Rachel running for the house.

"Vsevolod!" Brother's true name echoed through the fields. Forbidden. She'd forgotten again.

Rachel staggered the last few feet to Brother's workshop, which was heady with smells of sawdust and varnish. She found him bent over a chest of drawers.

"He's back." She started crying, which turned into a coughing fit. Brother had told her to stay in bed with the hot compresses, but she hadn't minded him.

He went to look out the window at the Sawbones approaching the house with his black bag in hand. "Stay inside and keep still."

She twisted her fingers in her apron and whispered, "He's coming for me."

"Hush." He petted her head, and then hailed the Sawbones in the yard.

Rachel watched through the window, catching snatches of the conversation.

"We didn't call for you," Brother said.

"I received another call from Mrs. Page, your neighbor. Seems she's concerned about your sister." The Sawbones tipped his hat back. "Was that Rachel I saw a minute ago?"

"This family doesn't hold with medicine."

"Then she *is* ill, your sister." The Sawbones waited. "I'd better take a look, all the same, young fella."

Rachel moaned and drew back. She knew what was in the Sawbones's bag. Brother had told her. Needles. Knives. A mallet for crushing bone. The Sawbones had left his card in the door last time, and Brother had fed it to the fire. It was doctors who locked Brother away, gave him a bum leg, kept him from the War.

She coughed into her hands, looking around the workshop. The old privy stood partly open. A picture was tacked to the inside of the door, one of those pinup calendar girls, with blonde curls piled on her head. Rachel's stomach tightened and she stepped away.

"Did you hear they found her without a stitch on?"

Good churchgoing ladies in hats and gloves, whispering together in New Ashford Sundries about the Awful Thing.

"God only knows what was done to her. Dumped along Old County Road like garbage."

"The sweater she was covered with? Tess knitted it herself."

A chorus of gasps.

One woman saw Rachel standing nearby, dismissed her with a glance.

Rachel ran through the workshop side door, through the

summer kitchen, into the house. Up to the attic floor where she hid her special things. Brother didn't know about them; he didn't like reminders of their old life. Sometimes she needed to touch things that had existed before, though; before the memory of Brother sitting in one of the parlor chairs in the New Ashford house, head hung low. How he'd gripped her to him and wept against her stomach for a long time. In his hair, she'd smelled a bonfire.

Raisa—her true name—opened the hidden door. Her favorite toy of all was wrapped in sailcloth, missing a piece but still sacred, from the time when she was small. She began coughing again. When she looked at her handkerchief, it was dark with blood.

Natalie awoke in the east bedroom. Two frosted windows allowed muted daylight.

She found Teddy sitting on the top step of the main staircase, hands dangling between his knees. He bolted upright at the sight of her. "Are you okay?"

"I think so. Did you come with me? Did you see?"

He shook his head. "You disappeared again, and I was holding air."

She went to the open attic door, hesitating. "We have to go up there. Raisa hid something that we're supposed to find."

Teddy took the flashlight out of their backpack. "I guess I don't have a choice. Right behind you."

The attic ran half the width of the house. The spiderwebs were epic, cathedrals of silk issuing from the rafters. There was a crawl space beneath the eaves, and the chimneys stood exposed at either end of the room.

Natalie stopped. "Look."

There was a small wooden door built into the side of the east chimney.

Teddy peered inside. "I've heard about these. It's called a smoker. People used them to cure meat in the smoke coming up from the fireplace."

Inside, two bars were suspended in darkness. A cast-iron pot dangled from a hooped handle, and Natalie worked the hinge free.

She set it on the floor and removed the lid, covering her hands in soot. Inside was a sailcloth bundle stained black. Inside that was a tin box stamped with Russian figures.

"Can you open it? My hands are all gross—"

Teddy was already taking off the top and folding back the wrappings. He withdrew a painted wooden doll with a dimpled face and a scarf tied under her chin.

"A nesting doll," Natalie said. "*Matryoshkas*—that's what they're called. It looks handmade, doesn't it?"

He popped the outer shell of the doll in half, removing each identical doll and lining them up across the floor. "Isn't there's supposed to be a tiny one in the center?"

"Her favorite toy, with a missing piece," Natalie said, turning the biggest doll over and finding the word RAISA scratched into the bottom in childish lettering.

"The name 'Rachel' was probably something her brother George—his real name was Vsevolod"—Natalie struggled with the pronunciation, "pushed on her. American, and forgettable. They didn't speak English with any accent, so . . . I don't get it. Maybe their parents were immigrants?"

The tin box also contained a few picture postcards, a pennywhistle, and a silver locket watch. Teddy lifted the chain until the locket dangled between them, winking dully in the glow of the flashlight. The timepiece had stopped long ago.

Natalie reached out and touched it, watching it spin.

"Vsevolod didn't want anybody finding these things." Her voice was hoarse. "I'm pretty sure he killed somebody."

CHAPTER 12

"You and me. Friday night." Delia socked Natalie's shoulder as they passed each other.

"Huh?"

"You're my date."

Delia took an order, and then came back, grinning.

"Big party at Passamaquoddy Lake. I don't want to go alone. Come on. Illegal bonfires? Night swimming? Boys—well, townies, but it'll be dark. You can pretend they have mystique in the dark."

Seeing the look on Natalie's face, Delia grew serious. "Nobody named Lowell or Jason will come near you. Promise. I'll make sure of it. They probably won't even show."

She glanced over at Teddy, who was mopping up a spilled milkshake, his hair hanging in his face. "You can bring him, too, if you want." She made a *huh* sound. "I've been working here for a year, and I've never been able to get more than three words out of him. Either he's the short, silent type, or he can't stand me."

"Teddy? He's not shy. He's just used to people not getting him, I think."

"You guys are really close, huh?"

Natalie nodded, watching her cousin wringing the mop into the bucket. "You know what? Night swimming sounds good. We'll be there."

"*Yesss*. We close together tomorrow. You guys can ride with me."

The house was waiting for them after work. Natalie stopped on the path.

"I can't figure out where Vsevolod's workshop used to be. Raisa ran down a long string of attached rooms, and then into the kitchen. Some of the house must've been torn down."

Teddy propped his hand over his eyes to block the sun. "Maybe that's where the door you drew on the wall went, the one you go through in your dream. Why do you think the house wanted you to know about it so bad?"

Natalie shook her head as they went inside, bracing against the cold. "Look." She pointed at the staircase.

Ice coated the banister and frozen rivulets ran down the stairs to the hall. Above, the ceiling light-fixture socket was crammed with icicles, like a mouthful of crooked teeth.

"The better to eat you with, my dear," Teddy said.

When the light came for Natalie, she didn't fight it.

AUTUMN 1948

Outside, the kitten was yowling. It had been three days since Vsevolod had gotten out of his sister's bed to do more than shuffle to the john, but finally the keening from the dooryard penetrated his grief.

His reflection rose in the vanity mirror as he sat up. A patch of daylight stretched across the quilt. Raisa's dolls lined the bureau, a row of sixteen little black shoes. He'd set them up like that while she was bedridden. Three weeks of listening to her drown. Then silence. The graveside service, the smell of wet soil and autumn rot. The only other mourners for Raisa had been that busybody from down the lane and her husband.

Outside, the kitten shrieked and climbed the doorframe.

Vsevolod made his way downstairs. The leg was stiff today. Days like this, he remembered the docs and all they'd done for him. The damn hospital, for his own good; the damn treatments, for his own good, electrodes pasted to his temples, coursing electricity. Waking in the infirmary with a cast on his leg, the Sawbones leaning over him as if he were the bigger man—*Sometimes the treatment results in seizures and a fracture occurs. A sound mind is worth it, wouldn't you say?*—though what he really meant was *Buck up, boy-o; you could be fighting the Japs right now.*

But Vsevolod's leg hadn't healed well. Good for a war story, at least, one he'd made certain Raisa memorized, even if she had a mind like a sieve. He was no 4-F. Nossir. He wasn't that type.

He looked down at the orange kitten sitting on the flagstone, tail curled beneath it.

"I suppose you think I should let you in." He grabbed it by the scruff—the thing had never liked him, and tried to claw his hand even now. He carried it inside and dropped it along the way, like a rolled newspaper he'd forgotten he was holding.

He got a fire going, ate a little, plucking thoughtfully at his lower lip. "A fellow can't abide loneliness," he said to the cat.

Loneliness was crouching behind him now, massive, smothering. He knew the remedy, and climbed the stairs again. The cat shot past him into Raisa's bedroom, where it stopped, tail bottle-brushing.

"What?" he said.

Its eyes were round and gleaming as marbles. Raisa's dying scent was everywhere.

Vsevolod grabbed the cat by the scruff, opened the window, and let it fly. He didn't watch to see where it landed. Then he continued up to the attic floor. His treasures were in the crawl space. He dragged the trunk out of its musty corner and opened the clasps.

Inside was a girl's hat. He pressed it to his nose and inhaled deeply. He'd snatched the tam before setting the girl's clothing alight in the woods that night. That New Ashford girl. Always going to the market with her two sisters, laughing to get his attention. One day, she'd walked home from the market alone.

Now he had her hat, and he'd been very wise to hide it even from his sister, who would never have understood. Raisa had suspected too much as it was. She was a child at heart; she couldn't understand how it was between a man and a woman.

Vsevolod gazed into the darkness of the crawl space, considering his bleak longing.

And then he knew how he would survive.

CHAPTER 13

"Raisa never left that house. She was still *there*. The cat sensed her." Natalie sat cross-legged on her bed, passing the *matryoshka* doll between her hands. "Vsevolod wouldn't get her help. The sickness was all here"—she pressed her hands against her chest—"whatever it was. Drowning her."

Teddy thought. "Tuberculosis, maybe? That was pretty common back then."

"And he spent most of World War Two locked up in a mental hospital. The war wound, his army background? All bull. Lies to make him look good. The inside of his head was . . ." She bit her lip. "Worse than blackness."

"He really murdered a girl in New Ashford, didn't he?"

"And then moved to Bernier to hide. End of the Earth, right?" Natalie shut her eyes. "He was making plans. Something bad."

"Nat." Teddy touched her shoulder. "All this stuff is over and done with. Remember."

When she didn't look at him, Teddy reached out and stopped her motions with the doll.

"I just don't get why this is happening to me. Why the house wants *me*, you know? I've never experienced anything like this. I'm about as sensitive as a rock. I'm probably the last person on the planet who can help."

"So. We get in even deeper." Teddy's expression was grim. "And hope we can get ourselves out again."

During supper, the house phone rang.

"Got it," Natalie said. "It's probably Mom and Dad."

She picked up the extension in the living room, perching on the arm of the La-Z-Boy. "Hi." She said it again as the silence stretched on.

There was static on the line, and for a surreal moment, Natalie thought it was the house calling. She sat up, eyes wide.

Then there was a small sigh, like someone swallowing their intention to speak. The connection broke.

Natalie hung up. The phone rang again immediately.

"Who is this?" she said sharply.

"Deb Payson. Who's this?"

"Oh! Mom, it's me."

"Nat? Why are you answering the phone like that?"

"Somebody called a second ago and wouldn't say anything." Years of dodging her parents' concern made her backpedal. "Probably a telemarketer. I think I could hear the call center in the background."

"Oh." Mom paused, sounding casual as she said, "So, how're things?"

Natalie gave the abridged, PG version. Yes, tips were better, and no, she wasn't homesick.

"What do you think about coming home for a visit this week-end, anyway?" Mom said.

"Weekends are crazy at the Grill." Natalie's mind raced with the repercussions of missing two whole days at the house. "I can't abandon Cilla."

"She won't give you one weekend off?"

"I'm not saying she won't; I'm saying I'd feel bad. I'm one of the only full-timers." Sweat prickled along her upper lip. "They need me."

Natalie could almost hear the sound of her mother's mouth shutting on the other end.

"You know what? You're being responsible, and here I am, ragging on you. Sorry, hon. Let me talk to Cill."

"Why?"

"So we can say bad things about you. Put her on, please."

After she handed the phone off to her aunt, Natalie went back into the dining room. Teddy hadn't eaten much, mostly pushed the food around on his plate. As Natalie sat back down, she said, "Oh, yeah. Tomorrow night after work, we're going to some party at Passamaquoddy with Delia. I forgot to tell you."

His eyes grew huge behind his glasses. "You said I'd go? You didn't even ask me."

"So what? You got a date?"

It was a joke, but Teddy groaned and scrubbed his face hard before standing up.

"What?" Natalie watched him carry his plate into the kitchen.

"What's the big deal?"

"I can't go. Tell her I'm sick. Actually—tell her I'm dead."

His footsteps pounded upstairs. A moment later, his bedroom door slammed.

Natalie ran through the dream tapestry, following a trail of foot-prints on a January day she knew too well. These were her Bernier woods, hers and Teddy's.

Down Pemaquid Road she went, to the big chestnut tree on the corner. The woods were still, but the girls whispered all around her, Raisa's voice now recognizable among them.

Teddy was waiting by the frozen brook, chin tucked into his coat collar, reading My Brother Sam Is Dead *and eating an apple, one leg dangling down. Natalie saw him exactly as he'd looked at twelve and a half years old, braces and all.*

Teddy saw her coming and smiled. That was when they heard the footsteps.

Jason Morrow was in the lead, as always, smiling in genuine pleasure. He'd found their hiding place. Much later, at the hearing, they would learn that he'd been searching for it since fall.

"Surprise," he said, as his friends caught up to him. Grace's tawny hair was yanked back in a braid, her face broad and high-cheekboned, her expression always placid, even when rabbit-punching somebody in the kidneys or chasing them between the shops downtown, throwing stones collected from the harbor beach.

Peter McInnis was a little out of breath, being the stocky one. Reddish hair with nearly invisible brows and lashes, a smile that showed metal fillings. Peter had actually been friends with Natalie and Teddy in elementary school—Cilla had babysat for him—but when sixth grade and hormones hit, he'd drifted away.

Lowell was tall and gawky-thin, with a smirking, watchful face; always the observer, good for holding people down while Jason punched. He didn't seem to own a coat, instead wearing a flannel shirt all winter.

Teddy stepped back, ready to bolt. Jason shook his head. "Uh-uh. Don't. I've got something you and your girlfriend are gonna want to see." His hand moved to something tucked into the waist of his jeans. "And you know what? You're both gonna eat it before we're done here."

Peter laughed. He was good at that.

CHAPTER 14

Delia peered out the windshield at the deer standing dead-center in the lake road, transfixed by the headlights of her '97 Ford Aspire.

"Should I honk at it?" She pressed the center of the steering wheel, and then punched it, to no avail. "Okay. Apparently the horn doesn't work now, either. Awesome."

Natalie bit her lip, trying not to laugh. "Yell at it."

Delia leaned out the window. "Hey! Deer!"

The deer's head shot up, and it raced away into the trees, its tail a white flag before it evaporated into the darkness.

"See, you don't need all those modern features. A horn, a radio, an E-brake . . ." Natalie drove her elbow into her seat, hoping to jolt Teddy behind her. "Does she?"

"Guess not." His voice was quiet from the backseat. When faced with Delia's excitement over the party—not that he'd spoken directly to her at any point, he'd been too busy staring at the ground—he hadn't had the guts to refuse to come after all. Natalie could tell he was still mad at her, though.

They reached a dirt parking area where Passamaquoddy Lake lay nestled among spruce and fir trees. The lot was jammed, and voices and laughter echoed everywhere; bonfires blazed along the shore. Natalie started getting nervous about introductions, then remembered what Delia was wearing and realized that no one would be looking at her, period.

Delia wore a black mesh shirt and a poufy miniskirt that looked like it was made from strips of laminated magazine pages. And her boots, of course. Delia smiled and said hi to all the people they passed, but never lingered; she was a couple years older than most of the crowd and certainly seemed to have her own style.

"Brews?" she said, grabbing a couple cans from a cooler on the picnic table.

To Natalie's surprise, Teddy took one, avoiding eye contact.

"Nah," Natalie said. "I'll drive us home."

"Good woman. I wouldn't want to total that baby of mine." Delia gestured to the shore. "Pick a fire, any fire."

Natalie looked around. Some couples were playing chicken in the water, girls sitting on their boyfriends' shoulders, shrieking, trying to push each other over. The contender on the left was Grace Thibodeau. Grace was strong, and as Natalie watched, she seized her competitor by the upper arms and took her down, smiling faintly as Jason maneuvered them back, crowing over their victory.

"As long as it's very far away."

Delia followed her gaze. "Oh, damn." She sighed, hands on her hips. "Well . . . it's a free lake, right? Let's go down to the other end."

As they started down the shore, Natalie glanced back. Lowell was here tonight, too. He sat in the sand, his forearm resting across the top of his bent knee, beer in hand. He'd been watching the couples battle in the water, but now he glanced at her. He lifted his beer in her direction. The ugliness of the scene at his house returned, and his small gesture shamed her. She nodded to him.

"Nat." Teddy caught the hem of her shirt, frowning at Lowell. "Come on."

Delia led them up a wooded embankment. The aromas of lake water and evergreen mingled as they continued down the path to a rocky clearing. "Hey, I remember this place," Natalie said. "The rope swing, right?"

"Best spot on the lake." Delia sat, yanking off her boots. She wore a black string bikini beneath her clothes, and with no preamble, she grabbed the rope dangling from a tree branch and swung out over the water, dropping with a whoop and a splash.

Natalie stripped down to her suit. "Come on," she said, as Teddy sat sipping.

"I didn't wear my trunks."

"I told you we were going swimming."

He shrugged. "Oops. I'll guard the drinks."

She put her hands on her hips. "I shouldn't even let you drink that. What if Cilla finds out?"

"I'll chew gum on the way home. Happy?"

"Whatever. I guess." Natalie swung out on the rope so quickly that she didn't have time to judge how long a drop it was; her surprised scream echoed across the lake.

They swam and splashed, and finally Delia yelled up at the ledge, "Come on in! What are you waiting for?" Teddy called back his no-trunks excuse. "So what? You're *wearing* shorts. Get in here or I'll drag you. Your choice!"

To Natalie's amazement, he actually took off his glasses and his shirt—truly, he was the skinniest boy she'd ever known—and plunged in after them. Huh. Apparently, Delia's opinion carried more weight. How long had Teddy been secretly crushing on her?

Natalie made herself scarce as Teddy treaded water, loosening up and acting more like himself as Delia chatted away. Natalie swam around the rocky outcropping, floating on her back and looking up at the stars. She willed herself to enjoy the peace and not let thoughts of the house intrude, repeating a mental mantra: *Don't think about it, don't ask "Why me," enjoy the moment.* After a while, she climbed back up the ledge and got dressed.

She noticed somebody wandering around at the base of the path. Lowell. She considered letting him poke around in the dark for a while longer, but, remembering his salute with the beer bottle, said, "Looking for me?"

"Yeah."

He didn't come any closer, and she finally walked down to him, standing with her hands in her back pockets, her hair hanging wet and snarled down her back. The firelight cast flickering shadows on the shore around them.

"I didn't expect to see you here," he finally said.

Natalie shrugged. "It's a free lake."

Lowell nodded, taking a long drink. He wasn't acting drunk, but his gaze wandered, and she wondered how many he'd had, seeking her out like this after she'd accused him.

"You didn't go running to your aunt with your crazy stories, did you?" He didn't give her a chance to answer. "Because I need the work at the Grill. It helps. Cilla's really gone out of her way for me."

"I didn't tell her anything."

He studied her face. A shadow of his usual humor returned. "Get any more surprises since you tried hanging the blame on me?"

"Actually, no. Which makes you look even more suspicious." His eyes widened and she held up her hands. "Kidding. I shouldn't have . . ."—she fumbled—"It wasn't fair of me to assume that it was you. I totally freaked out. I came into your house and . . ." She hesitated, and then said bluntly, "Sorry."

"I guess I've been accused of worse." He rocked back on his heels. "So, this shell you found . . . you're sure that it was the right type of ammo for a Browning Hi-Power?"

"It was from a handgun, not a rifle. That was all I could tell."

"Do you still have it?"

"Um, no. I threw it down a storm drain."

He blinked.

"I didn't want to scare my cousin or my aunt if I didn't have to. If they knew somebody left that for me . . . well, it wouldn't be good."

Lowell started to say something, thought better of it.

"Natalie, like you said. This isn't middle school anymore. If it were me—somebody leaves a shell on my doorstep?—I'd take it one of two ways: Either somebody's messing with my head, or somebody wants to take a shot at me."

Down shore, somebody shouted his name.

"There are some things you should know. Let's have that talk." He took a last swig from the bottle and tossed it into the sand as he turned. "I been meaning to get into the Grill anyway, take a look at the dishwasher. We'll catch up then?"

The same guy yelled Lowell's name again. Natalie folded her arms. "Better hurry. Jason wants to leave."

"I don't answer to him. We didn't come together, anyway."

Effectively silenced, Natalie watched him walk away. When she turned around, she found Delia and Teddy standing up on the ledge, watching her.

They came down to the shore.

"Did I witness the impossible?" Delia said. "Did you two bury the hatchet?"

Natalie glanced at Teddy. He stood there in his damp madras shirt and pleated shorts, his expression doubtful. "It's not that simple," she said.

"Why not? What aren't you guys telling me?"

Teddy was the first to break the silence. "Better sit down. It's a long story."

CHAPTER 15

Natalie was the first to speak. "Have you ever heard about a kid named Peter McInnis?"

Sitting cross-legged in the sand, Delia looked from Natalie to Teddy. "No-o-o. Should I have?"

"It's because she's new." Teddy's ears turned red as Delia stared at him. He tossed some pebbles into the fire. "We were on the newspaper together this year," he muttered.

"We were?" Delia shook her head. "Why don't I remember this?"

"Seniors don't usually remember sophomores."

"Oh." Delia toyed with the pop-top of her beer can. "Well. I hope you didn't think I was being a snob when I started working at the Grill. I would've said something, if I'd remembered you."

Teddy was doing his super-embarrassed *Rain Man* thing, rubbing his hand back and forth over the top of his head until his hair stood up, so Natalie said to Delia, "It must've been tough starting senior year at a new school."

She snorted. "Sucked. After my folks split up, my mom wanted to move back to this area. Her parents had a camp here when she was a kid, golden childhood memories, blah, blah, blah. Imagine my glee at the prospect of prom and graduation with total strangers." She gestured to her ensemble. "Bernier isn't exactly an ideal fit for me, anyway. Four-wheelin' and going to Dysart's at midnight."

Natalie smiled. "You can grow up in this town and still be on the outside. Teddy and I were. We had our little group of friends, but it boiled down to him being too smart, and me being . . . too weird, I guess." Natalie hugged her knees. "Like I told you, Jason and Grace and Lowell used to give us crap. They let Peter hang around with them, though. I think they respected him because he got into more trouble than they did. Even before he turned into a complete jerk, he was always getting sent to the principal's office."

"Remember when he flushed Mrs. Boudreaux's reading glasses and car keys down the toilet? Stole them right out of her desk during free period." Teddy laughed bitterly.

Natalie swirled a stick in the sand. "One day in January, Teddy and I were hanging out in the woods. Jason and the rest of them showed up, and Jason had this gun. He took it from his stepdad's closet. The guy's a vet, totally into weapons. Jason told everybody later that he only brought it along to show off. To scare us."

"Jesus," Delia said. "That's messed up."

"Yeah. Teddy and I ended up running into the woods."

A muscle worked in Teddy's jaw. "I don't care what Jason told the cops. He was planning on shooting somebody that day. It was just Peter's bad luck." Delia's eyes widened as he went on: "I ran east, back toward town. When I heard the shot, I ran even harder."

"I, like a genius, went the wrong way, deeper into the woods," said Natalie. "I heard the shot, too. It was so loud, sounded like it was right beside me." She hated the hazy, unfocused feeling of this memory, as if it had been stretched out of all proportion, to the point of translucence. "I remember trees. I got so lost. The woods went on forever."

"She didn't get home until dark," Teddy told Delia. "The cops and a search party had been out in the woods for hours, looking for her. I remember I was sitting at your kitchen table when you showed up, Nat. One of the neighbors was staying with me while your folks and my mom went to look for you. You were so exhausted, you fell on your knees when you came through the door."

They were silent for a moment. Most of the partyers had gone home. Theirs was the only bonfire still burning.

"So what about Peter?" Delia finally said.

"The cops found him by a gully, dead. He'd been shot once in the stomach. The bullet hit a major artery. He bled out in minutes." Natalie exhaled slowly. "When the cops went looking for Jason and the rest, they found them all at home, like nothing had happened. They all told different stories, too. Jason and Grace claimed Peter had taken the gun from Jason and chased after Teddy and me all on his own. They said they bailed after that, went home. Lowell said he got scared and left as soon as Teddy and I ran away."

Delia threw up her hands. "And . . . what? Peter accidentally shot himself?"

"That was the theory all three of them gave. And it probably would've gone over, too. But no gun was found at the scene. Should've been lying on the ground by Peter's body if it had gone off in his hands, right? Somebody was there when he was shot, and took the gun with them when they left. They didn't get help, didn't do anything. The state police tore the woods and all of our houses apart looking for that gun. Without the gun or a confession, they said there wasn't enough evidence to charge anyone with murder. Just a dead kid. And a town full of armchair detectives guessing whodunit."

"This is when your family moved away?"

"Yeah. I started freshman year in Lincoln two months late. My parents thought I was still recovering and kept me out. I testified at the hearing in Bangor that winter, and that was the last time I saw Jason or the rest of them until this summer. Couldn't get far enough away, honestly."

But then, in Lincoln, the dreams had begun, drifting down those silent hallways in the snow. Obviously, there was no getting away from Bernier, she thought.

Somberly, they got their things together and doused the flames. Natalie drove; the Aspire's stick handled like an International Harvester, and she was so focused on jockeying that she didn't see the person on the roadside until Delia said, "Oh, Lord."

Natalie recognized Grace, dressed in a camouflage tank top and cutoffs. She had a rolling sort of walk, her Converses dangling from one hand, a bottle from the other.

As the Aspire bumped over potholes, Natalie forced herself to say, "I can stop, if you want."

Delia shook her head. "You're driving."

"It's your car."

Teddy spoke at last. "She looks wasted."

Lips pursed, Natalie slowed. At least Grace was on Delia's side of the car.

Grace leaned into the window, hands braced on her thighs. Her wet hair was combed straight back from her brow, revealing a pair of dangly silver earrings glinting like lures. The tattoo on her arm was a colorful jumble of numbers and symbols. Natalie wondered how many hours she'd spent under the needle.

"Grace? You okay?" Delia waited. "Where's Jason?"

"Ah." Grace waved, sloshing Captain Morgan's. Her voice was low and smoky. "He's pissed at me again. Same old thing."

"He left you way out here?" Delia hesitated, sounding strained as she said, "Want a ride?"

Grace's gaze drifted to Natalie's face. Natalie didn't look away. There was something magnetic about the girl's wide-spaced, dreamy aquamarine eyes, completely unsuited to the rest of her; she didn't seem to be trying to intimidate Natalie so much as see straight through to the back of her skull. Finally, Grace pulled back. "Nah. I'm good." She gave her brief, shouting laugh. "Maybe I'll go howl at the moon or something." She thumped the window frame twice. "See ya, Dee."

"Go easy on that bottle, girl."

"Yeah, yeah."

Natalie watched the rearview mirror as they continued on their way. Grace Thibodeau's vague outline blended with the darkness and was gone.

CHAPTER 16

Delia lived a short distance from the Grill, so after they dropped her off with her car, Natalie and Teddy walked back to the Grill to get their bikes.

"What do you think? We've still got an hour before curfew." Natalie nudged Teddy. "We could ride out to the house and back in no time."

"Call me crazy, but I don't really want to go there in the dark."

"Well, me neither." The pull was relentless, overpowering any commonsense notion of dread. "But I also don't want to miss a day."

Teddy exhaled loudly. "Mom can't find out. She'd lose it if she knew we took the bikes out at night."

Natalie had a headlight attached to her handlebars, so she led the way down the back roads. There were no cars on the fringes of town at eleven o'clock, nothing but the singing of crickets and frogs and the occasional rustle of something nocturnal from the woods. On the way, without discussing it, they both braked in front of a two-story home with a garage sitting dark and silent among the trees. The owners must've gone to bed for the evening.

There used to be a sign by the driveway that read THE MCINNIS FAMILY, with ceramic donkey planters at each end.

"After Peter died . . . when did his folks move away?" Natalie said.

Teddy gave a small shrug. "Four, five months. His mother totally lost it. Mom said she drove past here one time and saw her sitting on the grass. Just sitting, staring into the woods. Like she was waiting for Peter to walk out of the trees."

He shook himself and trained his gaze away from the woods.

Inside the house on Morning Glory Lane, their flashlight lit up arctic patches of wallpaper and crumbling moldings.

"What did you and Lowell talk about tonight?" Teddy's voice sounded hollow in the silence.

Natalie didn't look at him. "Not much."

"Really? That's all you've got for me. 'Not much?'"

She shrugged uncomfortably. "Just . . . getting to know each other, I guess."

"Why would you want to do that?"

"I'm not saying we're besties now. But I don't think holding a grudge forever has done anybody any good, do you?"

He scoffed, shook his head. "Whatever you say."

As Natalie reached the left parlor, she stretched out her hand to open the door. It was enveloped in the light.

She sank into it.

AUTUMN 1948

By the time Vsevolod had shaved and dressed, the haze of English Leather around him was as suffocating as being locked in a tack closet in hottest July. A dollop of Wildroot Cream-Oil to fix the idiot kinks and whorls in his hair completed the look of a swell, out for a night on the town.

He entered the crisp evening. His '34 Dodge sedan coupe was black, gleaming with fresh wax. He hardly used it, save for occasional drives where he thought and planned and looked for girls. He gripped the paper flyer that he'd torn from a telephone pole—*Halloween Dance! Ten Cents a Head!*—and set off, jingling his keychain along with the radio. On the keychain hung a memento, something of Sister's that he'd taken when they were small.

It took an hour to reach the grange hall. The windows were bright, jack-o'-lanterns leering between the porch rails. Vsevolod parked on a side street and cut the engine. Strains of "One O'Clock Boogie" leaked into the night every time someone went through the doors. Vsevolod lit another Chesterfield.

The evening wore on. He smoked and waited. The final number played and the place began emptying out. It was only a matter of seeing which girl it would be. Some part of her could sense him coming, he knew it.

He drove up the road, trolling. A cluster of girls shrieked with punch-drunk laughter. A boy walked alone, fists thrust in his pockets. Farthest ahead, alone in the dark, was his girl. His blonde. She wore a green dress coat, and her hand rose like a pale bird's wing as she shielded her eyes against the glare of the coupe's headlamps.

"Hey, there," he called out the open window.

She moved closer, a small-town girl who'd spent a lifetime recognizing every face in every car window.

"I'm Bill, Bill Ebbins. Out of Blue Hill? Heading home from the dance. Gosh, I got myself all turned around here."

He'd gotten out a road map and smacked it now, making it crackle.

"Would you be willing to steer me in the right direction? I'll give you a ride home for your trouble."

Whatever she said in response was lost to him. What mattered was that her pale-bird hand was lowering, that she was passing before the headlamps, coming around to the passenger side door. Beside his trembling knee, his keychain, a tiny painted *matryoshka* doll, swung with dying momentum from a noose of string.

CHAPTER 17

It was nearly ten a.m. when Natalie awoke. Muzzy from bad dreams (*and lights flying*, she thought, *lights flying*, though the phrase was senseless), she stepped out of the summerhouse and found a note taped to the door. Teddy's square, precise handwriting read *Meet me at the library when you finally get up.*

It was hot outside, stagnant, but the library's air-conditioning did wonders for her disposition after the bike ride across town. She found Teddy at the microfilm machine in the reference room. He didn't look up when she dragged a chair over.

"Thought you'd never show," he said. "Welcome to research hell. They haven't transferred any of their newspaper archives online yet."

Natalie looked at the stack of microfilm containers labeled BANGOR DAILY NEWS 1948–1949, 1950–1951, and so on. "Wow. Find anything yet?"

"The librarian helped me." He held out a copy of a newspaper article. "November 2, 1948. I've been looking for anything else, any mention . . ." He pressed the rapid-advance button on the reader. Newsprint flew by.

With a constricted feeling in her throat, Natalie skimmed the article titled SEWALL GIRL MISSING. "Irene Godsoe, age eighteen. Disappeared Saturday, October 31, while walking home from the Sewall Community Halloween Dance."

Teddy dropped back against his chair, rubbing his reddened eyes. "The *News* never talked about her again. Trust me. I checked."

"We need more than this." Natalie thought. "If Sewall had a local paper back then, I bet they ran a huge story on it. 'Hometown Girl Kidnapped?' "

Teddy was on his feet, hunting down the librarian with Natalie at his heels.

"The *Coastal Reader*. Went under in the sixties." The librarian drew a bound volume marked 1948–1950 from a shelf with a sigh of exertion. "These books are all we have. I'm sure I don't need to tell you to be careful."

They pored over the bound *Coastal Reader* editions, facsimiles of the original newspaper pages enlarged to twice their size. Not much had changed in the world of local journalism over the last forty years: small-town politics, human interest stories, advertisements—only instead of plugging Hannaford weekly specials, these ads plugged something called Bile Beans ("Be Thin and Fit!") and pork loin for thirty-nine cents a pound at the local butcher. The date heading passed from summer 1948 into fall.

Irene Godsoe consumed the front page of the Monday edition. They'd printed her school portrait. Irene's hair was side-parted and pin-curled. She was cute but not exactly pretty, her face rounded with a receding chin. She wore a fuzzy cardigan sweater over a blouse with a Peter Pan collar.

The article described how her mother had called the police late Saturday night when her daughter never returned home from the grange hall three miles down the road. A boy also walking home from the dance had reported seeing a car stopped on Dunne Hill Road. The driver had continued on before the boy drew near. The rural neighborhood was canvassed until dusk on Sunday, but no sign of the girl was found.

Natalie studied the picture. In her mind's eye, Irene's hair bloomed into a pale yellow, her cardigan, periwinkle blue. Another borrowed memory. "Her parents had this picture hand-tinted. They kept it in a frame on top of a piano."

Teddy stared. "That's insane. You really do bring something back."

"It's totally real. Like being there." She kicked the table leg. "I *hate* this. We can't *do* anything."

"The house wants somebody to know what happened to Irene Godsoe, right? She never came home." He tried to catch her eye. "This has to be a key to what's happening at the house. Those girls calling out to you in your dreams . . . maybe Irene's one of them. Maybe she wants you to know the truth."

"What the hell can I do about it now? It's been forty years. How can I explain to anybody how I even found out that Irene Godsoe existed at all?" Feeling gutted, Natalie dropped her chin onto her folded arms, saying softly, "I wish I knew what I'm supposed to do next."

Lowell showed up at the Grill an hour before closing time, heading into the kitchen with his toolbox. Natalie worked with a nervous twist in her stomach. Maybe this "talk" of theirs was going to happen after all.

Lightning crackled over the harbor. The lights dimmed a few times, and customers began asking for their checks and heading home. Delia leaned on the counter, fanning herself with a napkin as she watched her only remaining table, a couple who had ordered nothing but bottled water and sat reading their respective newspapers in silence. "Couple of Rockefellers," Delia whispered to Natalie as she passed.

Lowell had his head and shoulders in the dishwasher when Natalie went into the kitchen to take off her apron. She took her time untying the strings, studying the knobs of his spine against the thin fabric of his T-shirt, the inch or so of blue plaid boxer shorts visible above the waist of his jeans.

He seemed to sense her and leaned out. "Hey."

"Hi."

He wiped his hands on a rag. "I'm about finished up here. You got time?"

"Some, yeah."

"How about we grab a cup of coffee." He followed her gaze to the Bunn brewer with its stale pots of decaf and regular. "Different . . . coffee. Somewhere else."

Natalie noticed that Bess was lingering by the soda fountain, watching them with interest. A hot flush rose in her cheeks, but Natalie tried to channel Delia. "You getting all this?"

Bess made a sour face. " 'Scuse me." She swished back out into the dining room.

Lowell smiled, picking up his tools. "Remind me to stay on your good side."

"Who says you're on it?" It felt so bizarre, sharing a joke with Lowell Emerick, but things seemed to be moving along with a momentum of their own now. She shifted her weight. "Let me check in with Cilla."

When Natalie awkwardly explained where she was going, Cilla blinked, stunned. "Well. I should drive you."

He came through the kitchen doors. "We're not going far. Just coffee."

Cilla looked at Natalie closely. "Okay. This once. But call me when you get there and when you leave. You two be careful in this storm. Lightning's nothing to fool with."

Lowell stepped over the threshold and held the door for Natalie. After a hesitation, she went through.

CHAPTER 18

Rain pelted down as Natalie followed Lowell to his pickup. She climbed in and yanked the door; it groaned but wouldn't shut.

Cursing under his breath, Lowell reached across her and together they slammed it. "Damn thing needs grease, but . . ." Their faces were very close, and he sat back, humming tunelessly as he started the engine.

The cab was a mess, scattered with tools and fast-food wrappers. Natalie's sneakers tangled in a set of jumper cables. "Thought I'd clean the place up for you," he said, deadpan, as they pulled out into the street.

"So I see." She pushed a Big Mac wrapper away with one finger. "Where are we going?"

"Dysart's." He glanced over when she gave a snort of laughter. "What?'

"Oh, nothing. Just something Delia said."

They crossed the suspension bridge that spanned the Penobscot River and drove north to the town of Hermon, and Dysart's twenty-four-hour truck stop. Lowell and Natalie didn't speak until they were seated at a booth, the thunder like distant cannon fire beyond the plate-glass window.

Coffee came, and Lowell stirred for a long time, the spoon clinking against the ceramic cup. "You should go home."

She stared. "You mean home-home? Lincoln?" She gestured to the coffees. "You could've told me to get out of town by sunset back at the Grill and saved yourself a buck."

"I'm paying, huh?" He smiled slightly. Sitting this close, she noticed that he had a small crescent-shaped scar on his chin. "This isn't coming out right. Cilla didn't know what she was doing, letting you come back to Bernier."

"She's been telling me to give you a second chance, you know."

He shifted. "Some people don't deserve second chances, though. Some people . . . I dunno, they're like hornets. They'll sting you a hundred times, they like it so damn much."

"You're talking about Jason."

He rested back, one knee protruding into the aisle. "I've been thinking about the hearing lately. How after you testified, you and your folks didn't stay for the sentencing. That's when I finally got it—that it didn't matter anymore, what happened to us. We'd changed all of our lives in one afternoon." He smiled again. Natalie thought it was one of the saddest expressions she'd ever seen. "I remember you wore this black dress with white dots. I'd never seen you in a dress before. You had your hair pinned back, and when you cried during your testimony, pieces came loose. You kept pushing them behind your ears."

"I was growing my bangs out. How can you remember that?"

"It's a hard day to forget." Lowell cleared his throat. "Everybody thought we should've had a murder trial, not some half-assed kiddy hearing. They still think it. But there's nobody left to keep the lamp burning. Peter's family's gone. Moved out of state. What happened kind of hangs over everybody. Nobody talks about it, you know?"

Natalie took a breath. She wanted to sound blasé, light-years beyond caring, but instead, her question sounded like something a little kid would ask.

"Why did you hate us so much?"

He rubbed his eyes with one hand; when he looked at her again, his expression was raw.

"Christ, Natalie. I didn't hate you. Or Teddy. I didn't even really know you. All I wanted was to look cool and keep my friends. So what if they were assholes. So was I."

"But not anymore?" Her tone hardened. "Because you're different now. A whole new person."

His gaze was challenging. "Yeah."

"So why the sudden change?"

"It wasn't sudden. It took work." She hadn't expected that, and he pressed on through the silence: "Seeing Peter get buried in a plot up at Oak Hill had plenty to do with it. Seeing his mom screaming and freaking out when the service ended, trying to go to the coffin. Peter's little brother and sister seemed like they didn't even know where they were."

"I didn't go. I'm surprised you did."

"Probably would've been smarter of me to stay away. Nobody was happy to see me there. But I felt like if I blew it off—if I couldn't even show my face—that'd be the end for me. I'd have to start believing what everybody said. That I was guilty. Maybe

I didn't pull the trigger, but I might as well have." He spun the spoon on the tabletop. "Nobody would have minded if you and Teddy went. You were never really suspects."

"No."

He went on. "Then there was probation, court-mandated therapy, community service. Should've sucked, but it gave me a reason to get up in the morning other than skipping school and seeing how much weed I could smoke. Got me thinking that maybe I could make a plan, you know, for my life. In a couple years, I'm applying to the diesel, truck, and heavy equipment program they've got up at EMCC."

"Oh." She hesitated, finished her coffee. "Well, good for you." She thought it would sound lame, but it didn't. She meant it. "Tell me why you think I should leave Bernier."

"That shell was a threat. You know who Jason blames for the year he spent in juvie? You and Teddy."

"He seriously didn't expect our parents to press charges?"

"You're thinking like a person who takes responsibility for what they do. We're talking Jason here. Every single thing he's ever done wrong is because of somebody else. You should hear him. If you and Teddy hadn't testified, if you hadn't run away from us that day—on and on. He's talked about doing crap to Teddy before, getting even, but he hasn't followed through. I figured he never would."

He watched her take this in, her grip tightening on her mug.

"Jason might act like a real badass, but compared to the guys in the state home, he was soft. Grace told me that four of them cornered him in a stairwell once. When they were done beating him, they threw him down two flights."

"God." The waitress came by to check on them, and there was another thunderclap. The lights flickered. "I didn't know. Does Grace blame us, too?"

Lowell shrugged. "Doubt it. She's not really like that. You know that when Jason was locked up, Grace used to take a bus down there every weekend to visit him, all by herself? He still treats her like crap. Cheats on her. She won't break it off. I dunno, maybe she thinks she's in love."

"Wonderful." The coffee was staging a revolt in her stomach. "And Jason has the gun. Either he shot Peter that day, or took the gun and walked away from him while he was dying on the ground. Why would anybody *do* that?" Her temper snapped. "Why are you still hanging around with him?"

"I'm not, really. Not anymore. What do you want me to say, Natalie? That I should've ditched him after everything went down? Sure I should've. I didn't. I was fourteen and gutless, and now I'm almost seventeen and Jason and I fight more than we get along. It's like he thinks we've got to stick together or something. Like we got away with murder and need to have each other's backs."

"What do you think really happened to Peter?" She saw how his body stiffened, but his gaze remained direct. "You must have a theory. I'd like to hear it."

"None of us had any reason to want him dead. That's all I know."

Silence settled between them. Natalie bit her thumbnail,

picturing Teddy's reaction to this news. Jason planning, Jason bragging about how he was going to *get him*. Get *them*.

"You okay?" Lowell said. Was it her imagination or had his hand moved, as if he was thinking about laying it over hers?

"No." She pulled her gaze away from his fingers, from the bones of his wrist and the smudge on his skin, a trace of oil or dirt. "I'm scared."

Drenched with rain, Natalie came through the front door and found Teddy waiting for her.

The stained-glass lamp over the kitchen table was on. Otherwise, the downstairs was dark, Cilla no doubt having retired to her bedroom with the latest Nora Roberts.

Teddy was reading at the table, a glass of soda at his elbow with all the fizz gone out of it. He took in her soaked appearance, unsmiling. "You should've worn a jacket." Headlights played across the far wall and were gone. "There he goes, huh."

"Cilla told you."

"Obviously." He sat back, chewing his lip briefly, watching her. "Have fun? Talk about old times? You know, if you two crazy kids ever want to tour Bernier Middle and visit all the places where he slammed my face into the pavement, I'd be happy to—"

"Stop it."

"You stop it, Nat." His voice was sharp, his face strained. "You can't possibly be this stupid. Think about it for two seconds. You

come back to town, and all of a sudden, after two and a half years
of acting like Peter never happened, like *I* don't even exist, Lowell
Emerick's falling all over himself to 'apologize' and make things
right."

"He's sorry for what he did. The way he treated us." She faltered. "I believe him."

"Don't you think it's more likely that he saw the possibility of
getting laid in his future, and decided to invest in a little ass-kissing?"

She stared at him, the only sound that of rain on the roof. "I
can't believe you just said that."

"Yeah. Well. Believe it." Teddy was slightly out of breath. "You
don't get it. They always shit on me, and they're still shitting on
me. Every time they pass me in the hall and look through me, like
it never happened, like middle school doesn't count or something.
You destroy somebody's life for three years, never pay for it, and then
they're just supposed to move on? No. I'm sorry, that's bull." He
shoved back from the table, crossing his arms. "That's total bullshit."

After a long pause, Natalie sat in the chair across from him.
"Yeah. It is." She waited for him to look at her. "I think . . . for
Lowell, anyway, he's ashamed of who he was. He doesn't like to think
of himself as somebody who did those things, and when he sees
you . . ." She lifted her shoulder. "Maybe it's easier to look away."

"Of course it's easier to look away. But people with consciences
can't do that, Nat."

She exhaled slowly, shutting her eyes for a moment.

"Look. Lowell wanted to talk with me for a good reason.

Somebody left something else for me in the bird hotel. I didn't tell you about it."

When she'd finished explaining about the shell casing and all that Lowell had shared with her that night, Teddy sat stiff and straight, his face drained of color.

"See? This is why I didn't tell you at first."

His voice was shaking. "Did you ever think that maybe the warning wasn't only for you? That maybe me and Mom could be in danger, too?"

"I didn't want to scare you. I thought I could handle it myself."

"Yeah. How's that working out for you?" He watched her wince. "We could've called the police. That shell might've gotten them to look into Peter's case again. Jason could be arrested right now."

"You don't know that. Look, I'm sorry, okay? Maybe there's some other way we can get the police to look into it—"

"Like what? Letting Jason blow one of us away?" His anger seemed to go out of him all at once, leaving him drained. "Whenever I see that scumbag, something inside me just—clenches up. And I'm right there, in those woods again."

She bowed her head, knowing exactly what he meant. A drop of rain slid from the ends of her hair to her knee.

"Why do you think I'm working so hard at getting into MIT, Nat?"

She met his gaze.

"Because it'll get me out of here. I want to go someplace where nothing makes my heart pound like I'm being chased. Where maybe

I really can pretend that all of this crap happened to somebody else."

There was a long pause. She said softly, "Should we tell your mom?"

He deliberated. "Not until we have proof. Since we don't have the shell, I don't think a barrette will be enough to make the cops believe that you're being stalked. But"—he held up a finger as she stood—"you have to move into the guest room tonight. No more sleeping out back by yourself."

"I was planning on it."

Natalie headed toward the hallway, and then turned back, not entirely sure of what she was about to say; Lowell's remark about the day of the hearing had shaken something loose.

"You know what? I think that barrette might've been mine after all. A long time ago."

"Really?" Teddy shook his head. "Why would Jason have your barrette?"

CHAPTER 19

They went to the house so early the next morning that mist hung around the overgrown yard, gave everything a dreamy, surreal look. Teddy let her go in alone this time, Natalie wandering through the frigid rooms until the light came, and washed everything away.

Autumn 1948

Irene lay in a forgotten place where the eaves met the floor.

The crawl space was about seven feet long and three feet wide, a shaft barely big enough for her to lie down on a pile of old quilts, the stink of the bucket a short distance from her head. He hadn't even given her toilet tissue. There was a small window set into the far wall, covered with a panel. Dim light crept in around the edges, enough to hint at the transition from day to night. She pounded her foot against the door until she grew tired of it and rolled over.

Wait. She held still, listening, eyes on the door. No. There hadn't been a footstep in the room beyond. He wasn't coming.

She breathed painfully through her damaged throat. She drew the name "Ma" on the floorboards with her fingertip again and again. It made her feel a little better. She sensed her mother with her all the time; sometimes, a faint touch on her shoulder before she slipped into a waking doze. It must be Ma, reaching out somehow, worried and scared out of her mind.

A mouse scuttled through the wall to her left, making a sound like water gurgling through rocks. Her home at 132 Elm Road was where she belonged, and she was sure she'd said the address clearly to the man that night after the dance: *132, right there on the left, the yellow house*, repeating it when he still didn't slow down. The man's profile had been lit by the dashboard glow. Suddenly he didn't look so young, or so handsome, and he was trying to hide a smile, as if this evening, this car ride, were all part of some swell joke. He'd touched flame to a second cigarette between his teeth and held it out for her in an abrupt gesture, making her flinch.

You want a smoke? I thought all sophisticated ladies smoked. Aren't you grown? He was laughing at her and she felt sick—oh, she felt so sick. *Aren't you all grown up?*

"Ma?" If Irene concentrated, she could feel her again. There it was, the faintest touch, but this time Irene smelled something, too. Someone else's body, not rank, but like a girl who was due for her Saturday-night hair washing. Not a hint of Ma's White Shoulders perfume at all.

Natalie threw up in the bushes below the kitchen windows. When the nausea passed, she sat down heavily in the grass, gasping, wiping her face.

"You okay?" Teddy's voice drifted over from the steps.

She stood and walked back around the house toward him, stumbling over the frame of a bulkhead wildly overgrown with weeds. Cellar doors. Natalie lifted her gaze to the attic windows. Sunlight gleamed there, blade-like.

Teddy stood on the steps in half shadow, half light. "Did he kill her?"

"No." Natalie sank onto the bottom step. "He's taking his time. She's alive." She told Teddy what she'd seen.

They were both silent. The whip-poor-will called from the fields.

"I've never felt anything so . . ."

She raked her fingers through her hair, staring at the path they'd beaten around the house. Yellow rattlesnake weed had sprouted there, as if marking their footsteps.

"It felt like it was me trapped in there with him. Nobody ever knew. That's the worst thing. Nobody ever knew what that sonofabitch did." Behind them, the house's doorway felt like an arctic cave. "Raisa's spirit—whatever you want to call it—was there with Irene. Like she was trying to comfort her." At once, she was crying, the fields blurring into green and gold. "I don't want to do this anymore. I didn't ask for this. If I'd known, I never—"

"You never would've come?" When Natalie lowered her head, Teddy rested his bony elbow on her shoulder. "You had to. The dream was making you crazy."

"But what's the point if I can't change anything?" She let her hands dangle between her knees, her stomach hollow and aching. "I can't help her."

CHAPTER 20

Teddy was shuddering. His face was waxen and chapped from the cold, his nose bloody where Jason had cuffed him. Jason's smile had vanished. His eyes, deceptively cornflower-blue like some wholesome farm boy's, held nothing.

"My stepdad showed me how to shoot, you know. I beat his ass in target practice now."

Peter snickered, the sound uncertain, his grip on Teddy's arm loosening, as if expecting to be told to let go at any moment.

Jason slid the muzzle down Teddy's jawline.

"You got a big mouth. Bet I could fit the barrel"—he pushed Teddy's chin up—"right in there."

"Stop!" Natalie lunged forward, but Grace pulled her back.

"Nah. Let's make it a contest."

Jason swung his arm out and leveled the gun on Natalie's face. The hole in the barrel seemed incredibly black, a spot of oblivion hovering before her. He pulled the hammer back. She could see something like detached disbelief in his expression, as if he was watching himself from afar.

"Jase." Grace spoke near Natalie's ear. "What—"

"Shut up." His gaze went from Natalie to Teddy. His voice wavered. "I'm gonna count to ten. And then I want to see how fast you two can run."

The house phone rang early. Sleeping in the first-floor guest room, Natalie groaned and flopped onto her stomach, shaking the dream away. Behind her eyelids, those scorched spots of light danced again.

The phone rang twice more and stopped. Natalie checked the clock. Five-fifteen. Not even Cilla was up yet. With a groan, she went into the kitchen and searched the fridge for breakfast.

The phone rang again. Hearing it this time, wide awake with her bare feet planted on the linoleum, sent ice water through her. Bad news came this early in the morning, and not much else. She went into the living room and answered.

No one responded to her hello. It was the same as last time—a bad connection, a human presence on the other end.

"Who's there?" She pressed her lips together, waiting. "Say something."

There was a soft intake of breath, followed by a clatter as the person put the receiver down hard.

Natalie was distracted at work all morning. She was distantly aware of Delia kidding with Teddy as they passed each other in the dining room, him smiling at the floor and shaking his head. Coffee, bacon, pancakes and waffles; the shift passed by in a blur until the moment Natalie glanced out the window facing Main Street and saw her sitting on the curb. Time ground to a halt.

Grace was hunched forward, swaying slightly, as if rocking

herself for comfort. She was watching the Grill.

Natalie went through the motions of work, never turning her back on the window for more than a second. Grace stayed at the curb, burying her face in her folded arms and then peering up again at people walking by. Finally, she stood and crossed the parking lot toward the entrance.

Natalie put down the tray she was holding. "Cilla?"

Her aunt looked up from the register, watching as Grace came through the door and walked unsteadily to a back booth, where she sat, facing away from the counter.

Delia came over to Cilla and Natalie. "Again?"

Cilla sighed. "See how far gone she is." She poured a cup of coffee and handed it to Delia, who grimaced and took it with her.

Natalie watched as Delia leaned in close to Grace to understand what she was saying.

"She's drunk," Natalie said, a little amazed. Cilla frowned in acknowledgment. "She comes in like this a lot?"

"Every few months." Cilla ran her finger down the phone-number list on the wall and began dialing. "Her folks have cut her off. Her grandmother will pick her up. Put in an order for some dry toast."

Teddy passed by on his way to the kitchen, looking back at Grace. "Really? It's ten o'clock in the morning, Mom."

"I can tell time, thank you very much."

Grace hunched over the booth in a sort of black stupor, staring into her mug. Someone played a tune on the jukebox, something twangy and full of small-town pride. The people who were sitting across from Grace paid and left, and, steeling herself, Natalie went to retrieve their tip.

She kept her eyes down as she scooped the bill into her apron pocket, but she felt Grace's stare on her like a physical thing. Finally, she returned it.

Grace's strange eyes were swollen and cat-like. One of her knees was badly scraped, and her Converses were muddy, as if she'd been walking through damp, shadowy places. Intimidating as she was, Natalie remembered the truth: how Grace was always the kid without lunch money unless she took it from someone else, who never had her homework done, who you'd see waiting for rides on any given corner, her expression making it clear that whoever she was waiting for, they probably weren't coming.

"You should've listened." Grace spoke barely above a whisper. She took in Natalie's incredulous expression and slowly shook her head. "To what I didn't say."

"What?"

Grace's mouth quirked humorlessly. "I tried telling you." She rested her chin on her folded arms and seemed to sink into a doze.

Natalie stood there. The phone calls. Of course it was Grace—those small sounds could've been made by anyone, but she could only hear Grace in them now, the quiet gasp, the swallowed need to speak.

"So tell me now. Grace . . . ? Hello?"

She wouldn't answer.

Natalie walked away, her steps gradually speeding up. She couldn't get far enough away from the girl, from her sharp junipery odor of liquor and sweat and melancholy. She went behind the counter, shaken.

It wasn't some sweet old lady who came for Grace. It was Jason. Natalie found it hard to imagine anyone's grandmother entrusting him with their flesh and blood, but there he was, stone-faced, jerking Grace's elbow as if she'd embarrassed him. Jason turned his glare, all 500 watts of it, on Natalie as he guided Grace to the door.

In the same moment, Natalie felt Teddy by her side. She'd never even heard him coming.

In the parking lot, Grace pulled free and shouted something at Jason that couldn't be understood through the glass. Jason tossed up his hands and got into his truck, revving the engine.

Grace watched him drive to the exit with her arms folded over her chest, seeming shrunken, somehow, and terribly young. The truck idled, and Grace ran to catch up, barely climbing in and shutting the cab door behind her before Jason gunned out into the street.

CHAPTER 21

Inside the house, ice had spread from the walls to the floor. Natalie found frost in a fine colorless fur over the metal fixtures and door-knobs. The kitchen sinks held a solid heart of ice; in one, the drain plug hung suspended. She closed her eyes as the lights came for her.

WINTER 1948

They were close enough to touch, but Irene knew he wouldn't. She sat on the floor in the attic room, listening to him breathe.

She'd awoken to find the door standing open. She'd sat up, fearing a trap, and gradually sensed him waiting out there in the room beyond. After an endless time, she'd moved toward the dim light.

Irene considered drawing herself to him now, begging. She could make herself do that. *Please, mister. Please.* She began to cry in small wheezing sounds. "Please." What was left of her voice sounded like a stranger's, tiny and cracked. "Let me—"

Fabric wafted over her face. She gasped, waiting for him to wrench it around her throat, but he didn't. Gradually, she found a neck hole, and then put her arms through. It was the pink dress she'd worn to the dance a hundred years ago.

He dropped her shoes into her lap; she'd hated wearing

them that night because the heels were scuffed, but Ma had said everybody would be too busy worrying about themselves to look at her feet. Irene lifted her gaze to his face and was directed back down, his large hand cupping the top of her head.

He helped her to her feet. It was over. He'd grown tired of her and now he was letting her go. He steered her out of the room. Behind them, the crawl-space door stood ajar.

A narrow staircase led down to a landing. Squares of dusky light spilled out of open doorways. The house had the feeling of being very large and very empty. Irene knew she had to be good, resist the urge to run, let him do this his way. She didn't want to spoil it, please God, no she didn't.

They came to a landing before the main staircase. From the corner of her eye, she saw someone. A slender girl standing in the last doorway with her hand resting on the frame. Irene opened her mouth. She might've burst with it—*He has another girl; I'm not the only one*—but in a moment that shape became less like a person and more like light settling over a piece of furniture, a certain angle of perspective. The peculiar rushing within her guttered and died.

Downstairs, they stopped in the foyer. He pulled on a coat, lit a cigarette behind his cupped hand. She spoke again in her rough whisper, "Are you taking me home now?"

The pause hung so long she believed he was going to ignore her as always. But then—"Yes."

115

THE DOOR TO JANUARY

That evening, while drying the supper dishes, Teddy said, "Anybody up for some poker? We haven't played since Nat got here."

Natalie said, "I'll get the change." Any distraction was welcome; the memories of Irene's last walk and Grace's cryptic words at the Grill ran through her head endlessly. *You should've listened to what I didn't say.* Followed by, *Are you taking me home now?* And Vsevolod had told Irene that he was. That was over sixty years ago. What had really happened?

Natalie set the change jar and the deck of cards on the table. "Let me grab my stuff from the summerhouse before I forget." She pointed at Teddy. "Then I'll be back to kick your butt."

"Keep on telling yourself that."

Natalie crossed the backyard, passing the bird hotel. Something on the periphery of her vision made her turn back.

There was a dark, smeared fingerprint on the lower left-hand corner of the birdhouse roof.

She stared at it, feeling her heartbeat swing into a low, bludgeoning pace. She reached out and lifted the lid.

In the dusky light, the object inside was indistinct, a bundle wrapped in fabric that might've been torn from an old T-shirt. Natalie poked it—it felt solid—and she lifted it out. Unwrapping flap after flap, compelled by some awful fascination to hurry as the fabric became saturated and the smell hit her nose, metallic and ripe, until she reached the moist center. Her gift was an assortment of small, veined organs in a jelly of blood.

The cop car in Cilla's driveway brought the neighbors outside to water their yards in the near-dark, craning their necks and whispering to each other.

Bernier was too small to have its own police department, so an officer had been dispatched from Bucksport, a young guy with a crew cut and a shave so clean it looked raw.

After the officer saw the bloody pile on the fabric and the fingerprint on the bird-hotel roof, he said, "You folks have any idea who might want to leave something like this?"

Natalie looked at Teddy. He'd stayed silent while they waited for the officer to arrive, but now he nodded to her. "Tell him, Nat. Don't leave anything out."

Cilla's mouth opened in disbelief as Natalie explained. By the end of it, her aunt's arms were tightly crossed, and every few minutes, she'd shake her head, looking off at the street.

The officer poked through the entrails with a pen.

"Well, it's not human, but you knew that. Looks to me like somebody gutted a small animal, woodchuck or raccoon, maybe. Miss, you've been sleeping in the summerhouse up until last night?"

Natalie nodded.

"Excuse me." He went back to his cruiser and spoke into his walkie-talkie.

On the verge of tears, Natalie looked at her aunt. She felt colossally stupid, a little kid who'd been gloating over her secrets. "Cilla, I am so, so sorry."

Cilla turned back, then pulled her into a hug. "Don't worry

about being sorry right now. Let's just get this figured out."

The officer came back. "I've notified Dispatch to send some help." He scratched the side of his nose, looking around. "We'll bag what we need, see if we can't get at least a partial print off the birdhouse roof. It's pretty smeared, but I wouldn't rule it out. We'll need statements from all three of you. Once we get a report written up, we can go from there."

"Are you finally going to arrest Jason Morrow?" Teddy said.

"I plan to have a conversation with him, yes." The officer nodded toward the summerhouse. "Anybody checked that out yet?"

"No." Cilla rested her hands on Natalie's shoulders. "I told the kids not to touch anything. Wasn't that the right thing to do?"

"You did fine." The officer went over to the summerhouse door and pushed it open, peering through the gap, and then jumped slightly when the three of them stopped right behind him. "Uh, folks, if you could stand back—" He hesitated, looking down at the step. "We've got some glass here." The bulb screwed into the exterior socket over the door had been smashed. The light didn't work anyway, but Jason didn't know that. Natalie gripped the hem of Cilla's cardigan. He'd wanted to leave her blind.

The officer opened the door the rest of the way. They all got a look at the inside, and Natalie groaned, covering her face. "Oh my God."

CHAPTER 22

The cops didn't leave until nearly ten. Teddy went up to bed early and Cilla was on her way, dumping coffee dregs down the sink.

Natalie sat in the living room with her knees drawn to her chest, watching TV without seeing it. She listened to the sound of her aunt moving around in the next room, and then went to the doorway and said, "I'll clean it up tomorrow. All of it." She dragged her big toe over the linoleum, tracing the pattern. "You'll never know anything happened."

"It's not important tonight." Cilla put away the sugar bowl. "And I don't want you touching any of that stuff without gloves. It carries disease, and we don't know where . . ." She gave her head another one of those stunned, helpless shakes.

Natalie blinked back tears. "But . . . Teddy's dad . . . I know he built the summerhouse and everything, and . . . I'm just really sorry."

"Oh, hon." Cilla pressed her palm over her eyes, seeming to mentally count to ten. "I wish you kids had told me what was going on. I don't know what made you think keeping something like that to yourselves was a good idea."

"Are you going to tell Mom and Dad to take me home?"

Looking conflicted, Cilla came over and smoothed Natalie's curls down with both hands, cupping her cheeks. "We'll talk about it tomorrow. Get some sleep."

TV was no comfort, and Natalie pulled the afghan over her legs even though it was too hot for it. She tried not to think about Raisa's things, which had been hidden inside a grocery bag underneath the cot and were probably smashed to bits now. Some darning needle she was. Some caretaker.

She wanted to be out on the nighttime roads with the breeze ruffling her hair, washing everything away, at least for a while. She didn't believe Jason would come roaring out of the dark to chase her down. Why end the game so soon, when he had them right where he wanted them, feeling small and scared, cat and mouse and all that? It would almost be a relief to deal with him face-to-face at this point.

Natalie went to the guest room and turned on the AC, shutting the door behind her. Hopefully it would look like she was inside, asleep. She knew where Cilla kept the house keys. Turning the lock on her way outside made this feel like less of a betrayal.

The grass was dewy, soaking her feet. She retrieved her bike from the shed and switched on the light between the handlebars, then took off down Bailey Street.

The ride did everything she'd hoped. The tension sloughed off as she pushed up hills and took corners, passing only two cars on the road the entire time. Main Street was a slumbering snake curving down to the harbor; many of the streetlights had burned out, but she caught a glimpse of the Quik Stop sign and realized that she must have a destination in mind after all. This was no aimless ride.

Loop Road wasn't far. It had to be nearly eleven o'clock by now, but the Emerick house was lit up, and there was music coming from the backyard. She'd only intended to pass by, take a look at the place, maybe think a little about the boy inside. But her desire to see Lowell surprised her. It made her walk her bike up the junk-strewn fieldstones and knock on the door.

Lowell came, the expression on his face softening as he recognized her. "Hey." He pushed the screen door open. "What're you doing here?"

"Is it too late?" Sliding her hands in her pockets, she glanced around. "I wouldn't have stopped, but it sounded like everybody was still awake."

"Oh, yeah. We're tearing it up tonight." His dry tone made her smile. "Dad's got some buddies over. Cold cans of PBR and horseshoes in the backyard. Kick-ass. Come on in."

She did.

"Sorry about the mess," he said as they went down the hallway, and then shrugged. "Ah, hell, you've seen the place. You know we're pigs."

They went into the living room. The local news was on TV.

Natalie sat on the couch, Lowell to her right, and the confession spilled out of her. "You were right. Jason's trying to scare me away." When she'd told him about the bird hotel, Lowell angled himself back, his gaze intense. "The summerhouse is trashed. More blood on the walls, and other stuff, gross stuff. Everything was thrown around and the sheets were ripped up."

"But the cops are going after him, right?" Lowell's tone was curt. When she nodded, he threw his elbow back on the cushion, saying under his breath, "Shit, Jase. You've done it now."

"I mean . . . what if I'd been in the summerhouse last night, like he thought? What would he have done then?" She swallowed. "Doesn't matter. I'm probably going home now, anyway." She was getting choked up and fought it, embarrassed, angry at herself. "It's scary, being here. Not like I remember. Or maybe Bernier was always like this, and it took Peter getting killed for me to see what was underneath."

She shut her eyes, picturing the hallways of the house on Morning Glory Drive, vaulted doorways opening into darkness, morphing into trees, black columns of forest twisting on and on. "I thought coming back here was something I had to do. Like a responsibility. I was an idiot. This place doesn't need me." She opened her eyes. "I can't change anything."

"I don't think you can change a place," Lowell said slowly. "It is what it is. All you can do is take yourself out of it."

She smirked. "You really want me gone, huh."

"No," he said without hesitation. "I don't. I think it'd be safer, yeah. But what I think you should do and what I want are two different things."

She stared back at him, warmth rising in her cheeks. "Thanks. I guess."

The music ratcheted up another notch outside, and he said, "Hold on." He went off down the hall, and moments later, she heard him yell "*Guys. Shut. Up,*" out the back door.

He was answered with whooping and laughter. The back door shut, then creaked open again, followed by an older guy saying, "What's up your ass?" He sounded gruff, drunk.

"I got somebody over. That's all."

"Girl?"

"Yeah, Dad. A girl."

When Lowell got back to the living room, Natalie was on her feet. "I should probably go. I kind of snuck out. Cilla doesn't know."

He walked her out. She started down the steps, but he stopped her.

"You call me before you leave town. Okay? We'll hang out or something. Don't take off again without letting me know."

Natalie looked into his eyes, for the first time noticing gold flecks around his pupils. "I won't." She lingered a moment, taking another step.

"Want a ride?"

"Nah. I'll be okay."

"You better."

Once she was biking down Loop Road, she glanced back. He still stood there, under the porch light.

CHAPTER 23

Natalie could hear them shouting behind her as the hunt began. The gun would go off any minute. The bullet would tear through her and she'd fall. But for now, she'd use every second.

She charged through branches and down an embankment. Teddy—why hadn't she followed him? Where was he now?

She hooked a left on a whim and ran, hearing Jason's cries of "Time's up! Gonna get you! Gonna get you!"

She'd been so sure she'd hear Teddy's footsteps or find the path he'd taken. There was nothing but trees. Someone crashed through the underbrush behind her, not far off, sending her racing in a different direction. She didn't know it, but she was zigzagging deeper into the wilderness.

There was a whispering sound moving through the air around her, filtering through the trees like a building gale. Maybe it was Jason and the rest, sneaking up on her? She pressed her back against a tree trunk and slid down into a crouch, gasping, straining to hear.

Footsteps. Drawing closer. Tears ran down her face. Someone cursed.

The whispers rose. Soft, feminine, unfamiliar. It was as if there was a chorus of voices around her, people she couldn't see. Even in her panicked state, she was able to glean one word, repeated over and over—

"Hide. Hide. Hide—"

Natalie broke from sleep. The dream had been so detailed, so immediate. How had she forgotten hiding among the trees like that, crouching and listening to the sounds of whispers and footsteps?

A tangle of spidery blue light flashed in the window. She gasped. When it didn't come again, she scrambled across the bed and looked out. There was nothing to see but the dark backyard.

Could someone have been shining a flashlight in at her? Jason, skulking around again? But the light had been too pulsating and strange for that, more like a cluster of fireflies. The yard remained still. Maybe it had only been some residue from her dream, a trick of her senses.

Natalie sat back, her thoughts turning unexpectedly to Lowell. Somehow, being with him for only a short while had helped to put things into perspective, helped stop that feeling of the ground sliding away beneath her feet. Funny, they'd sat together in his living room only a few hours ago. Felt like days.

Restless, she stayed awake for nearly an hour, staring at the yard. She could barely make out the shapes of the summerhouse and the bird hotel, black forms against a blacker night.

Her alarm clock went off at dawn. Yawning, Natalie grabbed rubber gloves, trash bags, and cleaning supplies, and headed to the summerhouse.

She'd hoped it might look better in the morning. It didn't. Standing alone in the doorway, she could feel the hatred lingering in the air like an electric charge, see it in the smears of animal blood across the walls.

Jason had dumped the bureau drawers and taken a buck knife to most of her clothes. The same blade had been ground into the top of the bureau in mindless patterns. The sheets were torn and smelled like they'd been pissed on. The only toiletries she'd kept out here were a stick of deodorant and a bottle of lotion, and both had been smeared on the floorboards and her clothes.

Afraid to hope, she righted the cot, expecting to see fragments of *matryoshka* doll scattered everywhere. The mattress had flopped off the frame, and she found the bag underneath it. Jason had been in such a frenzy that he'd slashed the mattress and moved on. Inside the bag, the doll and the locket watch were intact.

She started scrubbing, losing all track of time. A noise came from outside, and she found Teddy gathering broken glass from the step. "I don't want help," she said. "It's my mess."

"Too bad."

She ducked back inside and returned to cleaning the walls, glancing up when he eventually joined her. They worked together in comfortable silence.

When Cilla found them, the summerhouse was almost back to normal. She put her hand out to Natalie, touching her sleeve. "Want to talk inside for a few minutes?"

They sat at the kitchen table, the house full of the thudding of the washing machine as Natalie's few salvageable clothes cycled around.

"I'm scared, Nat. I really am. This isn't a safe place for you to be anymore."

Natalie's voice was hushed. "I know."

"You know that even if the cops come up with enough to arrest Jason, his mother will pay his bail? Patsy hasn't said no to that boy once in his life. That's why he is the way he is."

Cilla sighed and took her glasses off, looking at her niece with gray eyes the same shade as Natalie's own.

"This summer is really important to you, isn't it? Coming to Bernier. Facing those kids." She brushed some microscopic crumbs onto the floor. "I understand that you want to prove something. That's why I fought so hard for you when your parents told me that you wanted to waitress at the Grill."

Natalie thought of the house on Morning Glory Lane, with all its secrets still locked up inside. She thought of Lowell, how it felt to be near him.

"It'll look like Jason won," she said softly. "That's what he'll think, too. That he scared me off."

"I'm going to leave it up to your parents. Call them tonight and tell them what happened. Until then, we're going to change the way we do things around here. Don't go anywhere alone; remember to lock the doors behind you. I'll ask the police to have a car swing by at night and make sure everything's okay, at least until I hear from Sergeant Ward about where we stand with the investigation. I know you and Teddy have today off. Promise me that you'll stick together."

From the corner of her eye, Natalie saw Teddy's fair head bob past the window; she wondered how long he'd been out there, pretending to weed or water the garden. "I promise."

After Cilla left for work, she and Teddy did indeed stick together. They went to the one place, oddly enough, that felt safe today.

Morning Glory Lane.

CHAPTER 24

It was too cold now to stay in the house for long; Teddy waited outside again while Natalie took careful steps down the slick and icy corridor, letting the house take her where it wanted her to go.

⊕

WINTER 1948

Old Orchard Beach was a summer town, but tonight, lampposts burned all the way down the boardwalk pier.

The grand casino ballroom sat at the end, a double-decked funhouse wrapped with verandas that hung out over the water. Vsevolod joined the crowd bottlenecking at the ballroom entrance. The local radio announcer had made much of this holiday extravaganza, the ballroom opening for one night only to celebrate the season. Booze would flow. Girls would be out. A chance, after empty weeks. He had no choice but to see and be seen.

"Cigarette, sir? Cigar?" Some fleshy, nearsighted thing extended her box of wares from the strap around her neck. He registered milky cleavage, a sequined uniform, and moved on.

Evergreen garlands and strands of lights hung from the rafters, mistletoe from every veranda doorway. On stage, the orchestra was in full swing. Vsevolod ordered two fingers of Black

& White whiskey from the bar and went up the broad stairway, finding a shadowy place to survey the floor.

Did she ever feel it, that girl in scarlet velveteen with the silver tinsel pinned in her hair? As she laughed, jitterbugging with one partner and then the next, as she let them buy her glasses of rum eggnog and the room began to float . . . Did she ever pause to scan the crowded ballroom with a feeling of something amiss?

It was her hair. So fair it was almost white, styled in a Veronica Lake wave that he could easily follow through the crowd, especially with that bit of tinsel.

The orchestra dropped into "Moonglow." The sconces dimmed and the mirror ball began to rotate, sprinkling the room with light. The girl in scarlet was stumblebum and without a partner as couples brushed past her onto the floor. He made himself available. She held onto him like he was keeping her afloat.

Several drinks later, they were on the pier together, trailing a lively group of revelers who kept bursting into song. She murmured what a doll he was, treating her so nice.

"You don't mind taking me home? Straight shootin'?" She hooted suddenly, tossing her head back. "The old lady's gonna pitch a fit when she sees me."

"*Shhh*. Pleasure's mine."

"I don't gotta go straight home, you know. Maybe we could warm each other up." She giggled, stroking his lapel. Her fingernails were lacquered red.

"Edie!" someone called from behind them, making Vsevolod stiffen. But the cry didn't come again.

After they passed through the gabled entrance way, the girl's attention was drawn by the carousel off to the left.

"Oh, I used to ride that all the time. I had my favorite pony. What was her name? Th–Thunderhead, that was it." She grinned. Her left canine tooth was crooked. "If some other kid was on her, I wouldn't ride. I'd just stand there mad as a wet hen, watching them go 'round and 'round. . . ."

At the coupe, she slipped on an icy patch and went down. He caught two fistfuls of her coat, her sleeve separating at the shoulder with a purr of ripping fabric. A cheap goddamn coat, and she was unperturbed, laughing up into his face.

"*Whoop*sie-daisy, I didn't—"

He drove her head into the car door. Then he did it again.

She lay prone. Blood welled at the part in her hair. Making a frustrated sound in his throat, Vsevolod glanced around, and then carried her to the trunk.

Long drive home. Better get started.

The same tiny woman sat at the Historical Society desk. She smiled as Natalie put a dollar bill into the donation box. "Back again, I see. More probing questions?"

"Sort of." Natalie glanced at Teddy. "We heard that you have a collection of old photographs from around town?"

"Oh, you *are* gluttons for punishment. Superb."

She led them into a workroom and opened a closet containing half a dozen cardboard boxes.

"I'm sorry to say there's no secret system here. It's just a mess. We get more old pictures donated to us than we have time to organize, and most of them aren't of anything special—or particularly well-shot. But you're welcome to wade in."

When she had gone, Natalie opened their backpack and pulled out the article they'd copied at the library before coming here. It had taken some time, but they'd finally found who they were looking for in the *Portland Press Herald* archives, dated December 17, 1948.

There was a small faded photograph of the girl accompanying the article. Edith Anne Soucy, age seventeen, looked like a sharp-shouldered, square-jawed ghost, only her eyes—incongruously dark—well-defined in the exposure.

The article had run a week after Edith's disappearance. She was last seen on December 10 at the Old Orchard Pier Casino Ballroom, way down in York County. The only witness to come forward was her older sister Ruth, who worked at the ballroom as a cigarette girl. She and Edith had argued earlier in the evening about Edith sneaking into the party and getting drunk; later, Ruth saw her leave with a man and called after her, but her sister didn't stop. The assumption was that Edith had run away from home.

They didn't find any further mention of her in the microfilm. Just like Irene. Gone.

Natalie rubbed her temples. She should've known that Raisa and Irene weren't the only girls in Vsevolod's collection.

"Nobody made the link between Edith and Irene's abductions."

"They happened on different sides of the state. Two different kinds of girls," Teddy said. "Nobody was going to think a good girl like Irene was a runaway. It sounds like Edith was pretty wild."

"So she had it coming?"

Teddy stared her. "Wow. Not at all what I meant." She slumped over the table, and he eyed her. "Freaking out?"

"Just a little. A few days from now, I'm probably not even going to be in Bernier anymore, and all of this"—she smacked the article—"will be left—just—hanging. I mean, if I could at least give the cops an anonymous tip, tell them where to look for Irene's remains, anything . . . But all my coming here did was wake up the house. Now I'm leaving it behind again."

Teddy crossed his arms. "What do you think it'll do when it figures out that you're not coming back?"

"Get to me the only way it can, I guess. Through my dreams."

The search of the boxes took most of the afternoon. They found pictures of Main Street when it was nothing but packed dirt; the old sardine factory, still in its prime.

"Okay. Last box. Let's split it." Teddy was quiet as they worked. In time, he stopped. "Hey. What was the name of the family who sold Vsevolod the farm?"

"Leary, I think."

"Hey. *Hey*, look." The photo, taken from a distance, showed people clustered together in the dooryard of a connected farm building, the women distinguishable from the men only by the tent of their full skirts. Crabbed handwriting on the back read *Leary—Massy, Henry, Patience, and James, 1910.*

It was the house. A Colonial standing two and a half stories tall with twin chimneys and an ell branching off the east side, providing a passageway directly to the barn.

"This is it," she said in a hushed tone. "This is what we were missing. The door in my dream eventually leads to the barn. This is what the house wanted me to know."

"Why do you think that matters so much?"

"I don't know." She sat back. "It seems like sometimes the house gives us an answer before we've even asked the question."

CHAPTER 25

That evening, the phone call with her parents lasted nearly an hour. Dad kept asking her to repeat things, and Mom was so silent that Natalie wasn't sure if she was still on the line.

She actually considered telling them the truth about the house on Morning Glory Lane—for about two seconds—before she shoved the idea away. Her parents were commonsense types. They didn't believe in much more than attending Mass on Easter Sunday and playing the Megabucks lottery. They'd think she'd completely lost her mind, and all because they'd trusted her, this one time, against their better judgment. Wouldn't let that happen again.

Finally, Mom spoke the inevitable phrase: "Put your aunt on." Her tone was so icy that Natalie handed the extension over to Cilla without another word.

She went out on the porch, where Teddy sat on the swing, pretending to be interested in a book. She sat with him and they pushed the swing, not speaking until Cilla came out of the house. She looked at Natalie; the decision was written plainly on her face.

"How soon?" Natalie said.

"This weekend. Your dad's driving down on Sunday."

Cilla watched her lack of reaction, and then rested her hand on Natalie's head.

"It's probably for the best."

Taking in their grim expressions, she said, "Well—think. Saturday is the Fourth of July. You two can go to the fireworks, have a good time. It's been a long time since we've done that together." She watched them. "I'm sorry, kids. Wish it could be another way."

She went back inside, shutting the screen door gently behind her.

Teddy slapped his book down. "They can't do this."

Natalie thought of Lowell and the feeling that something was building between them, unexpected but right. She thought of Edith Soucy, locked in the trunk of the coupe, traveling through the winter landscape toward the house on Morning Glory Lane.

"They already did."

She stood up.

"Where're you going?"

"To call Lowell. I promised him I would."

She left him on the swing, staring.

After supper, Teddy biked to the Quik Stop to get a few things for his mother, and Natalie rode along, not wanting to sit around the house thinking about how she'd be back in Lincoln before summer was even half over.

As always, the line at the store was long. By the time they emerged with their purchases, the smattering of working streetlights had come on down Main Street.

Somebody stepped on the back of Natalie's sneaker, making her stumble. A flat tire: classic middle school move.

"Hey there, sunshine."

The bright tone was unmistakable. Jason peeked around her side, hands in the pockets of his jeans.

She stepped back, working her heel into her sneaker and hating the rising pitch of her voice. "Did you follow us?" She was aware of Teddy behind her, motionless, the grocery bag dangling from one hand. "What're you doing, watching our house now?"

Jason wore a T-shirt with a sleeveless flannel over it, the usual assortment of bracelets and rings. His pickup idled by the entrance, spilling some epic guitar solo from the windows. Grace sat in the passenger side, looking off at the street, one bare foot flat against the dashboard.

"I heard you had some trouble out at your place," Jason said. "Something to do with . . . birds?"

Natalie began walking toward their bikes again.

He fell into step with her. "Must've been serious to get the cops involved."

"Go away."

"They came to my house this morning and wanted to talk all about it." He smiled. The expression was vacant, like somebody was switching on a dim bulb. "I kept getting this feeling like they were waiting for me to admit to something." He shrugged. "I dunno. Anyway, they left after a while. Guess they must not have found much evidence or they already would've arrested somebody. They're really bad at that, huh?"

"You're disgusting." Natalie grabbed her bike, but Jason leaned against the siding, blocking her. A horn blared; Grace, laying her palm on the wheel.

Jason talked over the noise. "So . . . now you know. Anybody can walk onto your aunt's property and do whatever they want, whenever they want. Whoa." He widened his eyes and sucked air through his teeth. "Scary. If I were you, I wouldn't be sleeping so good right—"

Teddy slammed his hands against Jason's chest, knocking him back.

Recovering, Jason allowed himself to be pushed several feet away, his own hands raised. "Careful."

"Stay away from us." Teddy's voice was harsh and shaking. "You even talking to us right now is harassment. I'm going to tell the cops every word you said."

"What'd I say? I asked her how she was doing."

Teddy's face worked, almost too upset to speak. "Want another criminal threatening charge?" His words were a hoarse whisper. "Want to go back to juvie?"

Jason's smile broadened, showing dimples so deep they looked carved. Then he nodded, flicking his hand in a mock salute. "Bye, guy." He glanced at Natalie. "You're never happy to see me. I don't get it. I guess Lowell gets special treatment, huh."

The horn blared again. The engine revved as Grace worked the accelerator. "Come on," she shouted out the window. "Let's *go*."

By now the Quik Stop cashier had come over to the glass doors to gawk. Jason slid his hands back into his pockets and strolled off to his truck.

After he had peeled out, Natalie stared at Teddy. "That . . . was awesome."

"Really?" Breathless and wild-eyed, he wiped his palms on his pant legs. "I didn't think I could do it. I mean, I've *thought* about it enough, but I didn't think I actually could." He laughed a little hysterically. "But I did."

In the forest of her dreams, Natalie got down low, crawling on her belly into a thicket. The whispers softened around her, blending with the rustle of branches, the distant burr of a squirrel. Breathing shallowly, she tucked her arms and legs in close to her body.

The footsteps crunched, paused, headed off in another direction. Natalie risked a peek. Through a frame of leaves, she saw a muddy gully with a copse of birch trees on the far side. She caught a glimpse of dirty white Adidas.

"I say we call it." Peter, shooting for coolly bored but sounding more relieved, like the game hadn't been much fun after all. "They probably made it home by now. I know where they live—it's not real far."

Natalie shut her eyes and lay there, her pulse gradually slowing.

The footsteps continued on, but then, more curses. Both sets of footsteps circled back now, as if they were chasing each other.

Peter's voice, hitting the flat, bleating note it did when he was denied something: "Why not? You've had it the whole time. Come on. Just give it!"

Scuffling sounds. Swearing, a thud as someone hit the ground—and then the shot.

Natalie didn't have time to cover her ears. She was deafened by it.

Then she was up and running, flying forward before the echo had even faded. They could see her now, for certain, and she waited for the next explosion—the one that would bring her down.

CHAPTER 26

Lowell came through the Grill doors as Natalie was heading out back.

"You're early," she said, stopping. "And dirty."

He looked down at his dusty LaBrie Landscaping T-shirt, the knees of his tan Carhartts soaked through with damp soil.

"I'm not off work yet. I know we were planning to get together later, but I've got to go to a house we're working at in Bar Harbor to drop off some rosebushes." He jerked his thumb toward the parking lot, where his pickup sat, the bed loaded with bushes. "Last job for the day. Wanna ride along? It's pretty out that way."

Cilla was off making a bank run, so Natalie glanced over at Delia, who raised a hand. "Your shift ended three minutes ago." She added sternly, "Be safe, you guys. Remember. No extra stops."

"Damn," he said, "guess that means no Make-Out Point." Delia showed him her fist and he grinned. "We'll be good. Promise."

Natalie glanced at Teddy, but he kept his eyes on the table he was clearing and wouldn't look up long enough for her to wave good-bye.

She got into Lowell's truck and found her sneakers were resting on a floor mat. "The maid's been in," she said. Even the dash had been wiped clean.

Lowell tapped the new pine-tree air freshener dangling from

the rearview mirror. "Classy with a capital C."

She made an effort to put thoughts of the house behind her, and was successful for the most part. The memories would torment her tonight as she tried to fall asleep: Irene's fragile hope for a release that never came, Edith, dressed in red velveteen with blood trickling through her hair. And then the dreams of that day in the woods, dreams of Peter, so real and close that she couldn't believe she'd forgotten how he used to sound. But *this* was her life, right now, her afternoon, and she was going to enjoy it. She could have one little ride this summer that was all hers.

Lupines were in full bloom, pink and purple spears jutting up from roadsides and gardens. Lowell seemed satisfied not to talk, which was good, since Natalie wasn't up for making dazzling conversation, either.

He turned the radio on, and she hung her arm out the window, letting her fingers slice through the air.

It was a green day for the ocean, reflecting a deep emerald shade. LaBrie was landscaping for the owner of an enormous McMansion, the house a jumble of architectural styles, monopolizing a wide expanse of waterfront view.

Lowell worked in the side yard with three other guys while Natalie sat on the tailgate of his truck, swinging her feet and watching as they planted the bushes in twenty minutes flat, collected their tools, and split off for the day, the other guys casting curious looks back at her.

Lowell smacked his gloves together and tucked them into his

back pocket, looking at the house. "Cozy digs, huh?"

"If you like that sort of thing. You know, six bedrooms and the ocean in your backyard." She started sliding out of the bed and was surprised when he took her hand to help her down. It wasn't a long drop—she was almost as tall as he was—but she held on all the same.

"Not me." He walked around to the driver's side. "I'm gunning for a double-wide with a couple of pink flamingos by the door."

"Reaching for the stars, huh?"

He smiled a little. "Anyplace that's mine is all I need." He noticed her half-smile. "What? Do I sound like a loser?"

"No. You sound like Teddy."

Lowell laughed shortly. "Really? When I see him, I get the feeling he's trying to set me on fire with his mind."

"Probably." She hesitated. "You guys gave him a lot of shit in school."

He was quiet. "I said I was sorry for that."

"I know you are. Teddy doesn't."

"You're saying I should apologize to him? He'd want that?"

"No. I don't know." She rubbed her face and sat back. "I don't know what the right thing is."

They didn't speak again until they passed a sign for a roadside takeout. "I know we said no extra stops, but I'm starving," Lowell said. "What do you think? Let me buy you supper?"

"Hmm . . . if you throw in a chocolate shake."

After they ordered, he backed the pickup to the stone

143

embankment so they could sit in the bed and take in the view, a rocky ledge tumbling down to woods and then the ocean.

"So this is the famous Make-Out Point." Natalie took pity on him and laughed when he started to deny it. After a moment, she said, "I was wondering . . . why did you try so hard to make peace with me when I came back to town?" She watched him carefully. "I didn't make it easy for you."

He rested his forearms on his thighs. "Because. I hate what happened that summer before you left. I hate the way I used to treat people. And I hate that a screwed-up kid like Peter had to die for me to see what a complete waste I was." He looked down. "I like hanging out with you. I don't know many people I can really talk to."

She said in a tone not quite as casual as she'd intended, "What about Delia? You talk to her."

"Yeah. She's not going to stick around here long, though. She hasn't found her thing yet, but she will. Art, design, whatever. When she does, she'll move on and we won't see her again."

"Sounds like you've given this a lot of thought." She tilted her head to catch his gaze. "You don't have to stay in Bernier, either, you know."

"Sure about that?"

"What do you mean? You've got plans for school and everything."

"Yeah. Commuting. I mean, you live around here long enough, you start to recognize a lifer. It's like they're asleep inside. My dad.

He's one. My uncles. Jason. The old fogies you see in the Grill, day after day."

"And you, too? Come on."

She waited for him to laugh it off; when he didn't, her gaze dropped.

"It's because of what you said about the hearing, isn't it? When you decided that it didn't matter what happened to you anymore." She put her hand on his shoulder and shook it gently. "You don't give your whole life away over one mistake."

There was a burst of static as their order number was called over the loudspeaker. When Lowell returned with the tray, Natalie ate for a while before saying, "What if I told you that I've been having dreams about that day in the woods?"

"I'd say you're not the only one."

"I mean dreams that feel like memories. I think they're real."

"I don't get it."

"That day, after I ran away from you guys in the clearing . . . All I could remember were trees. On and on, forever. Something always felt weird about that, sort of . . . hazy. I figured my brain checked out for a good reason. Trauma, whatever. But there's more than that." She closed her eyes. "I remember hiding now. I heard people coming, so I crawled into some bushes. I heard Peter talking with somebody, saying Teddy and I had probably made it home and he wanted to give up the search. Then I heard him asking for the gun, like he wanted a turn holding it. Then there was the shot, and I ran."

Lowell stared at her, his burger forgotten. "You saw who shot him?"

"No." He was waiting, and at the last second, something kept her from saying *But the dream isn't over yet.* She knew what finding an eyewitness could mean for Lowell. Suppose it didn't go that far? Suppose her memories cut off as suddenly as they'd begun, leaving him with nothing but more questions? "No, I didn't see. I ran."

They ate in silence, only broken when Natalie offered him some of her shake.

When Lowell spoke next, his usual warmth and his grin were back.

"Hey. You're leaving this weekend. I probably won't see you again."

She started to argue, but he stopped her, wearing his slantwise smile.

"Can I ask something, then?" She nodded. "Can I kiss you?"

She made a sound of disbelief. "Seriously?" Heat washed over her, and then her argument with Teddy in the kitchen came back in vivid detail. "Why?"

"You really need to ask?" Lowell continued looking steadily at her.

With the slightest hesitation, she kissed him first, not feeling the full shock until her lips were on his. His hands slid over her back, one running up under her shirt and pressing against her skin, and she moved into him. He smelled of sweat and cut grass.

When it ended, she leaned against his chest for moment, finally lifting her eyes to meet his, the tips of their noses almost touching.

"I guess I've been wanting to do that for a while," he said, brushing her curls away from her brow. "How about you and me going to the fireworks on Friday? We can wait until then to say good-bye."

Her answer was a kiss.

Later, the frigid breath of the house unfurled from the back doorway as she and Teddy stopped together on the step.

"It could be him, you know." His voice was flat.

She looked at him, somehow sure that he knew, could see Lowell's kiss printed on her. "What?"

"You don't know for sure that Lowell didn't shoot Peter."

"Yes, I do, actually. You haven't talked to him like I do. He hates what happened to Peter. He could never keep a secret like that."

"He could be trying to find out what you remember from that day."

"So which is it? He's using me because I'm a girl, or because of what I know?"

"Any reason it can't be both?"

"Okay. We need to stop talking about this now. It's none of your business."

Teddy snorted, held up his hands. "Fine. Believe whatever you want."

"Thanks for your permission."

For once, she was almost glad to step into the cold and leave him behind.

Winter 1948

Dreams allowed Edith little rest. The walls of the tiny space closed in, breathing like bellows. Hands strained for her in the darkness, small, girlish hands, longing to make contact. She always cried out right before the fingertips touched her face.

There came the rattle of the lock, the scrape of a hand against wood. She was fairly sure she was awake—*or was it another bad dream?*

A square of light expanded in the wall, and she knew he was back.

Edith screamed as he dragged her forward by her ankles, hefting her up and over his shoulder. He carried her down a flight of stairs now, jouncing her. Edith fought, tearing at his neck with her fingernails.

Door hinges squeaked. They stepped down, and the temperature dropped sharply. They were moving through a dim passageway of rooms that smelled of sawdust, firewood.

Edith groaned. "Let me go . . . put me *down*, goddammit . . ."

He took her out a back door into the cold, fresh air. Snowy fields stretched out to the left; beyond that, woods. They were skirting along the rear of a big connected farmhouse, and the barn loomed ahead. He edged down a slope to the back of the barn, where he finally dropped her.

She scrambled back in the snow. He watched her, hands resting on his thighs as he tried to catch his breath, his great coffee-brown eyes shiny and intent. A dark-featured, husky fella. When she looked at him, he smiled.

A brief struggle; she tried to get away, he dragged her back.

"I see you," she shouted as he grabbed the front of her dress, pinning her to the ground. *"I see you now, you sonofabitch!"* She hit and kicked him anywhere she could as he took a key from the pocket of his tartan coat to open a lock hanging from the sliding door to the barn basement.

Stench gusted out. Old manure ran beneath a sharper, fouler odor. He pushed her inside, shutting the door as she attacked it. The lock snapped into place and she stopped, swaying, as his footsteps faded away. *"I'm gonna kill you!"* She punched the door once, sobbing.

She turned to face the darkness beneath the barn floor. The basement ran the length and width of the barn itself. Light seeped in through the spaces between the planks above the stone foundation and she could see that there was junk everywhere, old barrels, busted blueberry baskets, rope.

Edith shivered uncontrollably. *Think.* Cold wasn't so bad; hunger, either. Maybe this was only a punishment, something to break the fight in her. Couple hours, he'd be back.

"Smarten *up*," she whispered. "Think about what you need." Water, for one. She'd never been so thirsty.

Edith stumbled over the other girl, who lay nearby in a fetal position.

The girl had been so cold in the end that she'd drawn her

arms inside the bodice of her dress and dragged her skirt down over her knees. She remained frozen that way, cocooned. As Edith stared, her vision adjusting to the darkness, the contrast of the girl's pale dress seemed to glow like phosphorescence. The girl's eyes were partially open, opaque as dusty stones. Most of her upper lip had withered away.

Edith howled. She threw herself against the door, bounced off, and lunged again. This continued until she passed out.

CHAPTER 27

Natalie ran for miles through the woods, cutting through the wilderness along the town line. Fear and shock drove her on as she stumbled over fallen trees and roots. They'd shoot her any moment now. They were right behind her.

She emerged into an overgrown field and stopped, gasping, sick with exhaustion, disoriented with panic. Insects droned. There were no cars, no sounds of human life.

A house and a barn stood on the hill across the road, crumbling and surrounded by a dark mass of brambles. She recognized it, yet still didn't fully grasp that she was on Morning Glory Lane now, way across town from home. What she saw was a hiding place. She ran for it.

Thorns scratched and prodded her. She could smell the old house stink from outside, mildew and wet rot. Someone was whispering to her on the wind again. Natalie looked up to the attic windows. The sunlight winked there, viciously, hurting her eyes.

Natalie went around the house (worlds away, her sleeping form shuddered, resisting, trying to wake up) and looked at the back door. A padlock hung from the latch. She kept circling the building, pushing through the weeds.

A door in the lower half of the barn stood open. As she looked over at it, she understood at once that this was where the whispering was coming from. Deep down. A soft, imploring call—not a voice, exactly, *more an impulse. As if a good friend were waiting inside, peering out and wishing she'd come in so they could see each other better.*

She went over, standing at the doorway for a moment, head cocked, listening. The expression on her face was smooth, disconnected. She went inside.

Natalie snapped awake to late-night TV.

She sat up on the couch in the dark living room, running her hands through her hair. The gaping barn basement still yawned in her memory, a black maw, inviting her in. And she'd gone in. God, had she *forgotten* that she'd been inside that barn, of all places? Not possible. The memory had been taken from her, somehow, stripped away like old paint.

She registered Teddy's form in the easy chair. They'd stayed up late, talking about Irene. Maybe Vsevolod had choked her first and thought she was dead before he hid her away, but she wasn't. Or maybe he didn't care. They talked about everything but Lowell, a subject that was now most definitely off limits. They both must've dozed off.

The TV flashed as a commercial began, filling the room with light. Teddy was awake. His eyes were wide, and he was gripping the arms of the chair so hard the fabric was bunched between his fingers. His gaze was fixed on a space above her head. She looked up.

Three balls of brilliant light hung in the air. She shrank back. The lights moved with her. Hovering, blinking softly. Waiting.

Teddy's mouth barely moved. "Hold still."

After a moment of apparent indecision, the lights drifted, scaling the wallpaper and then the ceiling, twining around each other. They were hot white at the center, with auras of blue. They sank down in front of Teddy. His stunned expression was bathed in their glow.

The lights arranged themselves in a circle and spun above his nose, casting reflections in the TV and the glass face of the clock on the wall. This went on for an unknown period of time, the whole room charged with something like ozone. The air crackled with it.

Then, with sudden purpose, the lights rose. They merged, joining into a single pulsating globe. Something old and craven stirred in Natalie. She knew what came next. God help her, somehow she did. She cringed against the couch cushions with a shriek as the light shot forward, heading straight for her.

The overhead lamp burst on. Teddy stood at the switch plate. "Are you *okay?*"

Footsteps thudded down the staircase. Cilla appeared in her robe, her eyes swollen and bewildered. "What's wrong?" She ran to the front door, peering out through the curtains. "Is somebody trying to get in? Did you see somebody?"

For a second, neither of them could speak.

"Everything's fine," Teddy blurted. "We were horsing around, and Natalie yelled. Sorry."

Cilla took one last look at Natalie, who couldn't summon a response at all. "Oh. Well." After a long moment of consideration, she turned and went upstairs again, pausing once to glance back. "Keep it down, okay?"

When Cilla disappeared back upstairs, Teddy sat back on his

heels. He spoke in an awed tone. "Did you feel it at all?" She shook her head, speechless. "They flew right at you."

Teddy turned the light off again, satisfying himself that their visitors had really left, and then turned it back on.

"You were dreaming. Twitching around, making noises. I looked at the TV, and when I looked back at you, I could see them." He swallowed. "Hovering."

She spoke. "I was having my nightmare."

"It was the same light that comes from the house, Nat. The blue light? I could feel them looking at me. *Thinking* about me."

"Me, too." Like living things. "I think . . . I've seen them before. I saw a light in the bedroom window a few nights ago, a reflection. And sometimes, after I wake up, my eyes feel like I've been staring into the sun even though I just opened them."

She rubbed her chest, feeling tenderness there.

"What the hell are they?" Teddy asked.

She didn't have an answer.

CHAPTER 28

Another early-morning trip to the house, neither of them speaking much. It was the last place Natalie wanted to go. The only place she could.

✠

WINTER 1948

We go on here.

Edith put her hands over her ears, pushing forward, memorizing the circumference of the basement and all its obstacles. Broken mason jars, tipped chairs, piles of rotten cloth. She'd found an old canvas which she wrapped tightly around herself like a cloak.

She'd walked all night long as cold air filtered through the foundation. Her movements were the herky-jerky shuffle of a windup soldier, but still, she walked.

We go on here. The dead girl spoke in a cool, fathoms-deep voice. The words reverberated inside Edith's head like two people speaking at once. *You needn't fight so hard.*

"Be quiet." On each circuit, Edith gave the dead girl a wider berth, but her gaze was inevitably drawn to her oyster eyes, the protruding row of her upper teeth. The girl's feet had begun to curl inside her dancing shoes. "I'm not gonna die here."

Dead Girl wouldn't dignify that with a response. She let Edith try to walk out the hours. Had to be early morning by now. There was some light under the door. Edith had lived to see it because she was smarter, tougher. The dead one hadn't even looked for anything to keep her warm, probably hadn't checked for anything edible in those mason jars or felt the stone walls for trickles of ice to lick. She'd curled into a ball and surrendered.

Now look. The face that sank a thousand ships. Edith uttered a hoarse bray of laughter and continued tottering in her circle.

The corpse read her thoughts. *We're waiting to hold you, Edith. In time.*

"Like hell."

She slammed her toes against a chair without any sensation of pain, stumbled, and had difficulty getting back up. That this should be the final place she'd ever see, a frozen pit ripe with the scent of manure and rot, made her want to fly at the door again. Maybe if she kept moving. It was becoming much harder now.

Natalie returned to the present in the dining room, but horror drove her down the hall, past Teddy, who had been waiting on the back steps in the sunlight, trying to stay warm.

She dug in the weeds until she unearthed a stone. With a cry, she threw it at the house. A windowpane shattered.

She threw another one. It bounced off the clapboards. The

next one managed to destroy what was left of the window at the southern end of the attic.

Teddy watched her as she finally staggered back, out of breath. Eventually, she gasped, "She's going to die. She'll freeze." She shook her head, fighting back the images. She'd never be rid of them now.

Natalie walked toward the path, lost in pain and anger, until she realized Teddy wasn't behind her anymore. She glanced back and saw him standing on the path, the wind ruffling his shaggy hair and wrinkled polo shirt. She knew what he was going to say.

"Can you feel them right now? The lights?" When she didn't answer: "Do you think they're always inside of you? Or do they come and go?"

"I don't *know*."

"I was thinking . . . maybe they *are* the dream." He held her gaze. "Maybe they're your link to this house. You felt it. Those things were alive. Maybe they're pieces of the girls' . . . energy . . . whatever you want to call it. Raisa, Irene, and Edith. Maybe you carry them with you."

She tried to laugh but could produce only a choked, anguished sound.

"Nat. We need to go into the barn." He held her gaze, almost in tears himself, shaking his head as she backed away. "You saw it in your dream. You told me. You went inside the barn basement that day and something happened to you. Something changed you."

"No!"

"Yes! We've been looking for an explanation. This could be

it." His voice broke. "We're running out of time. Two more days, and you're gone."

She shifted, glancing over at the barn, sagging on its foundation. Her voice shook: "Would it make any difference if I told you that I really, really don't want to go in there?"

"Me neither." He came over to her. "I'll go with you. As far as they'll let me."

Together, they went to the basement door. The top hinge had corroded, and they had to drag it open across the weeds.

There were no skeletons, nothing like that. In fact, what they could see of the space was empty, the junk cleared out and hauled away by subsequent owners. Spiderwebs streamed from the dry-stacked stone walls. It wasn't as dark down there as Natalie expected; holes in the rotten floor let daylight stream down from the collapsed roof.

They went in, where cold seemed to suck the air from their lungs, crystallizing into white clouds in the air. There was a faint creak, and a rustle, an exhausted old elephant of a building on the verge of final collapse.

The light came from Natalie as it always did, but this time, it was her own past that was waiting for her.

January, Two and a Half Years Ago

Fourteen-year-old Natalie Payson stepped onto the dirt floor of the basement. There was a cavernous feeling and a mineral odor, an inescapable chill. She may as well have been miles beneath the ground.

She looked back at the doorway of light behind her, listening. No footsteps crunching through the snow, no sound of Jason or the others closing in on her. She began to understand how much ground she had covered. The figures she'd imagined still chasing her through the woods had been phantoms. No one could find her here. No one could possibly know where she was.

Something whispered in the darkness. A voice, or a mouse scuttling across the dirt floor?

"Hello?" Natalie called.

The darkness seemed to hold its breath. When she turned back, the door was closing.

Panicking, she ran for it, throwing her hands out to stop it as it slammed with such force that it knocked her back.

"Hey!" She yanked the handle, crashing her head and shoulder against the seam of gray daylight. No give. She shrieked and battered her fists. "Let me out!" It couldn't be Jason and the rest of them—they'd be laughing by now, teasing her.

She swiveled to face the blackness, gasping. Darkness ruled. More whispers, more hissing. Alone, yet not. Some primitive part of her understood now that she'd been baited here.

A bluish speck appeared in the far corner of the room. Several more became visible, flakes of light drifting out into the blackness of the room. For a moment, it looked like it was snowing in the basement.

Natalie's hands went limply to her sides. She walked toward the lights, all resistance gone. The specks settled on her hair and skin and seemed to dissolve, gleaming dully beneath her flesh. She put her hand out and touched one of the falling specks. Even through her gloves, it felt like a splinter of ice.

Distantly, she became aware that her feet weren't on the ground anymore. She hovered in the air, powerless to move, to speak.

Pain. She went rigid with it. Her brain impulses leaped and sizzled as the light washed through her, brutally plumbing her fourteen years' worth of memories. Images flew before her mind's eye—Mom, Dad, Cilla, and Teddy, her house, her school, moments of pain, joy—and then the intruders pushed further, beyond what Natalie had the power to know. Her body seized violently in midair. Spittle bubbled at her lips, hands clenching and opening.

When it was over, Natalie's body dropped to the frozen floor.

She stirred slightly. Only three spots of light remained now, dancing in the air above her like fireflies. They whisked over her chest and sank.

Hours passed. Natalie awoke. A bar of fading winter light stretched across the floor from the now-open doorway. Outside, a bird twittered.

Natalie's memory had been stripped. *Go home*, something inside her whispered, a new voice, a cold conscience. *Go.*

She crawled up the steps toward daylight. She'd bitten her

tongue, and she was wet, cold. She'd wet her pants like a baby, and that confused and frightened her more than anything, sent her running through the yard toward the lane without looking back. She cried in a blank, lost way as she ran, but by the time she'd finally reached home, she was empty.

Night had fallen, and when she saw her mother's bright kitchen through the windows, she headed for it, the memory of the barn basement and the walk home erased. She saw Teddy sitting at the kitchen table. She pushed through the door and her legs gave out, spilling her onto the floor.

CHAPTER 29

A bird twittered beyond the basement doorway.

Natalie emerged, breathing deeply of the fresh air. Teddy was just outside, waiting for her.

Shakily, he said, "Did you see it? What did they do to you that day?"

Natalie shook her head. She wanted to get on her bike. She wanted to pedal away from here and never look back. What good would it do, she thought numbly.

The house lives inside you. It is you and you are it.

"They looked inside me," she said stiffly, remotely. "I don't know what they saw. Something they liked."

After a pause, Teddy said, "Or something they needed."

That evening, Natalie found she couldn't sit still and went outside, wandering around the yard. Teddy's bedroom light was on, where he'd been since after supper, no doubt taking his frustrations out on his latest model. Or maybe hiding from her, avoiding the cloud of bad memories she seemed to wear like a shroud?

Natalie went over to the summerhouse and sat on the step. The bird hotel was gone; she and Teddy had pulled it out of the ground, hosed it off, and put it in the garage for the foreseeable future.

She glanced around to make sure no one was watching, and then touched her breastbone, roughly the area where the spirit lights had sunken into her. There should be *something*, shouldn't there, some clue, heat, or sensation? What happened to them once they were inside her . . . did they dissolve, coursing through her bloodstream like specks of fool's gold in a river? Bits of souls, carried inside her.

"Are you there?" She poked again, feeling ridiculous, and gave up.

Cilla appeared around the side of the house, her hands in the pockets of her jumper.

"Nice night." She sat beside her on the step and gently bumped her shoulder. "It's going to be all right, you know."

Natalie laughed hollowly, looking at her. "What is?"

"Everything."

"What makes you so sure?"

"Experience." Cilla folded her hands, and Natalie noticed for the first time how weathered they were, the skin creased from years of filling whatever role the Grill demanded, from prep cook to toilet scrubber. "Bad times feel like they'll last forever. Then they pass, and you're on to the next thing."

Natalie tried to imagine this summer behind her, and couldn't. She didn't seem to have a future beyond the house anymore, or a past before it. It had insinuated itself into her life, trickling through the cracks in her memory. She didn't realize her aunt was still speaking until she heard her say Peter's name.

"What?"

"I said it's crazy the way things turn out. Kids you've known since they were babies can grow up to be so lost, right here, in a place they've lived their whole lives." Cilla shook her head. "I used to watch Peter after school sometimes, when he and Teddy were in kindergarten—do you remember that? Your grampie was still running the Grill then, and I was waitressing mornings, looking after Teddy in the afternoons, doing some babysitting. Peter came here for about a year or so." Cilla gave a sad smile. "He and Teddy played together."

Natalie looked at the hole in the ground by the summerhouse again.

"Did Teddy ever play the game with the bird hotel when Peter was here? You know, leaving secret messages inside, playing spy?"

"Probably. Birds have never wanted to nest in that thing. Maybe it's too low to the ground." Cilla swatted at a mosquito. "Anyway. Kids. They break your heart."

"Is that why you're so nice to Grace? Why you don't bust her for coming into the Grill drunk?"

"I don't see how calling the police on a sixteen-year-old girl who's only hurting herself will do a bit of good. Everyone knows how she lives. Stays with one relative for a few months until she burns her bridges there, then off to the next one. Grace Thibodeau hasn't got a pot to piss in or a window to throw it out of most of the time, and the only reason she clings on to that"—for a rare moment, Cilla's disgust was evident—"*Jason*, is because she doesn't believe she deserves any better."

Elements of the story were so similar to Lowell's that Natalie felt chilled.

"Do you think Jason was telling the truth when he said that the cops don't have enough evidence to arrest him?"

"I think he was trying to scare you two. We were right to give Sergeant Ward a call about it. We'll get a restraining order, make sure Jason can't bother this family anymore."

They were both quiet. In tandem, their gazes went to Teddy's lit bedroom window. Natalie pictured him bent over his desk, trying to lose himself in the construction of an X-wing fighter or a '68 Mustang, trying to forget all they'd seen.

"I know you kids have been through a lot," Cilla said quietly, as if she'd read her mind, "but hon, you've lost that light in your eyes. I hardly recognize you without it. During all the trouble you and Teddy dealt with in middle school—the police, the hearing, the gossip—I never once saw you like this. Can't you tell me what's eating you?"

Natalie ducked her chin, afraid that if she looked at her aunt she might lose what little control she had left. She released a shaky sigh, listening to the crickets.

"Sometimes . . . I get the feeling that nothing ever really ends. Things come around and around again and we keep playing the same parts, doing the same things, hoping for a different turnout." Her voice choked off. "But it's impossible. You can't change the ending."

Cilla thought for a while. Her expression was solemn in the twilight.

"I'm sure it feels that way to you now. But your grampie had a saying that I try to remember when I'm scared and the world seems upside down. This, too, shall pass." She kissed the top of Natalie's head. "From what I've seen, it always does."

CHAPTER 30

Natalie's descent was slow. She flew, buffeting on cross breezes. Below, a house floated in a sea of field and forest. Her dream had come full circle.

She went down the corridor as snow sifted down from the ceiling, passing a moon-faced clock, a rack with a mirror. Swing music played softly from another room.

At the end of the corridor, the kitchen doorway glowed. Natalie went inside.

China covered every surface. Plates and bowls, teacups and saucers, all brimming with snow. On a woodstove sat a kettle. The steam from the spout had crystallized into ice.

Natalie turned to face the door with six panes of glass. As she moved closer, she heard whispering. "Natalie," the girls' voices said. "Natalie."

She opened the door.

They were out there, the trinity, suspended in the abyss with light streaming from them. What they were—their most elemental selves—could not be comprehended by the living, and Natalie screamed, and was ashamed.

"What do you want from me?" she managed to say.

Their energy blended and separated, impressions of Raisa, Irene, and Edith all palpable, sensed, not seen. Their voices grew guttural. "We wait for you."

"Why?" As Natalie stared into the abyss, air stirred around her face

and neck. Teasingly, at first, lifting strands of her hair. She knew what
came next.

"We wait. We spin the wheel, we make the thread." A ripple
passed through them, maybe a laugh, maybe a sigh. "We wield the
shears. We cut."

"I don't understand." Pressure grew around her throat.

"Cheated, all of us." Edith came through most strongly, with a
crackle of ozone and rage like heat. "Almost your time now."

"Almost time almost timealmostimealmost—"

"Teddy, wake up. Please wake up."

Light filled the bedroom and Teddy stared at her from the
cocoon of his blanket, his hair sticking out in corkscrews. It was
two a.m. Rain spattered against the window.

Natalie stood there, her face colorless and pinched, arms folded
tightly over her chest. She didn't remember climbing the stairs to
his room. She was crying too hard.

Teddy kicked off the sheets. "Downstairs. Before we wake up
Mom."

They went into the guest room and shut the door. Natalie
dropped heavily onto the bed, hugging the pillow to her chest. It
was a long time before she spoke.

"I get it now. Why the girls chose me. Why they waited all this
time for me to come back to Bernier. They knew I would."

She shifted her gaze to his bewildered expression.

"I'm like them."

"How?"

"They all died young. Before their time."

How well she was functioning, how clearly she was speaking; part of her still refused to believe it, clinging to childhood reassurances that bad dreams don't come true.

"When they looked inside me—that day, in the barn basement—they saw my past. Then they went further, right? They saw my future, Teddy. They know what's going to happen to me. They practically spelled it out for me in my dream tonight."

"You're not making sense."

"They've been waiting for me to come back this summer because they know I'm going to die here."

Teddy pulled back as if slapped. She got to her knees, still clutching the pillow.

"Maybe they sensed it the first time we biked out there when we were kids, the first time I got close to the house. They *knew*. That's why they lured me into the basement that day. To take a closer look."

"That's crazy."

"Crazier than seeing the past? Crazier than a house freezing over in June? This is why I'm different, Teddy—why I'm the key to what's happening. I can carry those spirit lights inside me because we're four of a kind. They can show me the past because of—I don't know, the common thread we share. Never meant to grow up."

"Jesus, Nat, don't *say* that!"

"Why shouldn't the girls be able to see a person's fate from beginning to end, if they wanted to? They saw something in my future that they needed. The spirit lights and the dreams were their way of communicating with me while I was out of reach."

"*Stop it.* You had another nightmare, that's all. You're reading too much into it—"

"You know better."

He shook his head furiously. "That's it. You're not going back to the house again. I won't let you. What's the worst it can do, give you more nightmares?" He stared at her. "Quit looking like that! You are not going to die!"

He smacked the alarm clock off the bedside table and it bounced across the floor with a reproachful clang. They both stared at it.

"You think . . . it might be like . . . a trade?" His voice was soft. "Your life for theirs, something like that?"

"Nothing seems impossible anymore. But whatever it is, it's going to happen soon."

"I won't let it."

"Teddy—"

"*No.*" He was glaring at her, struggling not to break down.

An odd sort of calm came over her. She knew what she knew. At least she wasn't alone in it. The girls were there, and always had been. It was her responsibility to reassure him, with a rock in her belly and cold sweat trickling down her back.

"Maybe you're right. Let's get some sleep. We can talk about it in the morning."

Sullen and unspeaking, Teddy claimed the extra blanket and pillow and made his bed on the floor, where she listened to him toss and turn, ensuring that nothing came creeping in through her darkened door. In time, he surrendered to sleep.

When Natalie's spirit lights emerged before dawn to explore the room and its occupants, neither of them woke.

CHAPTER 31

It was as if, eons ago, the weather gods had decreed that henceforth every Fourth of July would be drizzly, humid, and hardly fit for fireworks—in Maine, anyway. Natalie wasn't surprised to see raindrops clinging to the window screens when she awoke the next morning.

Teddy was gone. She heard sounds of breakfast being made in the kitchen, the coffeemaker burbling. Natalie yanked the sheet over her head and lay there, eyes closed, breathing shallowly.

Too much like being inside a casket.

She got up, showered, and dressed, packing her few remaining belongings for Dad's arrival tomorrow. Then she went out to the kitchen to join her family. She couldn't hide from whatever was waiting for her, and wasn't it just possible that Teddy was right— that she'd misinterpreted the girls' dream message? Wouldn't it be ludicrous to hide at home, acting like Chicken Little waiting for the sky to fall?

Her reflection looked grimly back at her from the mirror, unconvinced.

There were hollows under Teddy's eyes, and Cilla fussed over him, feeling his forehead for fever. Every time his gaze met Natalie's, the knowledge was there between them, and he almost seemed to flinch away from her. He left for the Grill on his bike with hardly a word to either of them.

Cilla went out on the porch and watched him disappear down the street, her hands on her hips.

Natalie spent the day with her aunt, playing Scrabble, reading in the yard, making lunch. At noon, the pounding of a brass band echoed up from Main Street, distant sounds of the Independence Day parade. A strong feeling of unreality persisted, a sensation of time rolling faster and faster. Natalie didn't believe she could slow it down if she tried.

Dusk fell swiftly, like someone dimming a lamp. She sat on the porch swing and waited for Lowell. He parked along the curb and came up the steps, taking his hat off.

"You look pretty."

"I do?" She looked down at her usual T-shirt and shorts.

"Always." He touched her cheek. "You okay?"

Instead of answering, she put her arms around him and kissed him. It was sudden, but neither of them let go for some time. She felt cheated. Was it possible to mourn for a romance that never really got started?

She slipped free. "Let me tell Cilla we're going now."

She went into the kitchen and hugged her aunt from behind, who, surprised, hugged her back. Cilla was packing the old wicker picnic basket.

"You and Lowell can ride with me, all right? I want to keep track of everybody tonight. And if you see Jason, steer right clear, understand?"

"You know that Teddy is catching a ride over from the Grill with Delia, right?"

Cilla glanced up. "*Well.* You could knock me over with a feather. A month ago, he'd have turned bright red if I even said her name."

The park was overflowing with people toting blankets and lawn chairs, the PA system on the bandstand cranking out a local country station. Hamburgers and hot dogs were cooking, and kids were running around in packs, shrieking and swirling sparklers through the smoky air.

As Natalie followed Lowell across the green, she noticed Grace, sitting alone on one of the boulders along the edge of the parking lot. People flowed around her without seeming to see her at all. She was picking at a scab on her knee, but then she looked up, watching Natalie from beneath her brows. Natalie tucked her arm through Lowell's and turned away, glad when she could no longer feel the girl's gaze on her back.

Cilla picked a good spot, and they set up camp.

"Hi!" Delia said, appearing in the crowd, followed by Teddy. They sat down on the blanket. "I'm so bummed. I can't believe you're leaving me tomorrow." Delia bonked her head on Natalie's shoulder. "What am I supposed to do?"

"Start making Bess a friendship bracelet?"

Delia elbowed Teddy. "She's running off to enjoy her summer. You and I are stuck back here in the salt mines."

"I beg your pardon," Cilla said, passing out sodas.

"Hey. I'm not laughing." Natalie plucked at the blanket. "I'm going to miss you guys like crazy." She didn't return Teddy's gaze right then because she knew she'd only start crying. She didn't want their last day to be like that.

The next hour could've been a snapshot from Natalie's childhood: the scratchy recording of the National Anthem blaring across the park, the fireworks booming overhead, the crowd cheering. For a time, Natalie cleared her mind of everything but the feeling of Lowell's arm around her, the showers of color in the night sky, and the belief that everything was okay, okay, okay.

The applause ended, and everyone started packing up.

"Can we ride with Delia?" Natalie asked. She saw her aunt's concern. "Just so we can say good-bye. We'll be right behind you."

"Well . . . okay. Be safe," Cilla said, glancing back a few times as if to be sure they weren't planning on lingering.

They got on their way, the moon hanging full and fat above. The radio droned a lullaby. Delia took the usual back roads. There were no streetlights, only the very occasional glimmer of lit houses through the trees.

They were coasting downhill when a parked pickup truck emerged from the darkness, stretched sideways across the lane. Delia swore and cut the wheel hard to the right, the passenger-side tires thunking into the ditch.

Delia managed to stop, slammed the car into PARK, and got out. "What the hell?"

They all walked over to the truck. The cab was empty.

The knot of tension that had been tightening inside Natalie seemed to snap, leaving her feeling weightless and untethered. Distantly, she thought, *Oh God. Here it comes.*

There was a rushing of footsteps from the woods—a shout—and then two shadows spilled through the trees onto the grass.

Natalie cried out as a Maglite shone directly into her eyes. Through the aura of light, she recognized them, too. Jason, holding the light. Grace, holding a gun.

Grace came around and kicked Teddy in the back of the knee, making him fall. She caught his shirt and propped her foot against his lower back, pressing the muzzle of the handgun to the back of Teddy's head.

"Okay." Her gaze leveled on Natalie. "Let's do this."

CHAPTER 32

Jason moved his pickup out of the road, and now it sat facing them, headlights burning. The radio played something howling and heavy.

Jason took a hunting rifle from the rack and rested it against his shoulder. The night seemed to have shrunk, as if there was nothing beyond this roadside and the six of them.

"Here's what you're going to do," he said to them, pacing unsteadily; he looked drunk, out of it. "You're going to get in the back of the truck. Grace is riding with you. You try to bail out, she'll shoot you. You scream or come at her, she'll shoot you."

Lowell's face was washed white in the strange light. "Are you guys crazy? Put the guns away!"

"Aw, shit, did I forget to tell you? We"—he gestured to Grace—"got a reunion planned. Eighth-grade reunion, right here, tonight. Us five are the only ones who got invites, and Dee wasn't even around back then, but hey. What do you want on short notice?" He watched Grace, who was still breathing on Teddy, gun trained. "Back off, babe," he said softly.

Grace shook her sweaty hair out of her face, her expression one of belligerent anguish, eyes swollen from liquor and tears. Natalie knew the gun in Grace's hand, recognized it. Whispering to herself, Grace stepped away from Teddy, who sagged.

Lowell's fists were clenched. He looked like he was barely restraining himself from rushing Jason. "You really did it. You walked away from Peter when he was dying. You took the gun, and you left him there. Why?"

Jason threw the rifle butt against his shoulder and pretended to fire with a *ppppow!* sound, making them all cringe. He laughed, shrill and cracked. "Damn, you guys are jumpy." He waved them toward the truck bed. "Go on. Move it. It's reunion time."

"I'm not doing anything else you say, you psycho," Delia said quietly. "So whatever you're planning, it's not going to work. Let us go home."

Grace came up behind Delia and shoved her so hard she stumbled.

"Stop it!" Teddy shouted.

Grace shoved again, and Delia wheeled on her. Teddy got between them before they could clash again, blocking Delia with his body as Grace lifted the gun to the level of his chest. He stared, eyes huge, breath hitching, and didn't move.

"Okay!" Natalie put her hands up. "Okay, we're all going. Come on, you guys."

Her vision pulsed with black spots as she climbed into the bed of the truck, flattening herself back against the frame as Grace got in beside her, holding the Browning Hi-Power casually, like an extension of her body.

Grace wore the same clothes she'd had on at the Grill the other day, a black camisole and running shorts, the outfit rumpled and dirty, as if she'd been sleeping in it. She smelled none too fresh, either.

Natalie shut her eyes, remembering sneakers crunching through the undergrowth, hearing Peter's voice echoing in these woods. *You've had it the whole time—come on.*

Was this what the house had seen in Natalie's future? A truck, a gun—a shot?

A pit of dread yawned inside of her, and she pressed her hand over her mouth, crying silently, not caring if Grace saw. The other girl only watched her with numb fascination, her hair spiking around her face in a sort of fairy's cap. There was dried spittle at the corner of her mouth.

They took a logging road through the trees that hadn't been used in years. Occasionally, the tires lost traction and it seemed they might get stuck—they all waited tensely then, exchanging looks—but Jason backed and filled and kept on going, deeper into the woods, bumping over ruts and washouts.

At last, they stopped. They got out and walked the rest of the way, single file, Grace occasionally jabbing Lowell in the back with her gun.

Lowell jerked around. "You want to keep that thing away from me?"

"Be quiet," Teddy muttered.

"Screw that. You for real with this, Grace? What the hell's going on? Why are you helping him?"

She wouldn't answer, only stared morosely back.

"Are you hearing me? What're you guys on?"

"Lowell, bud," Jason said from behind them, raising his rifle again, "if I were you, I'd shut up. Right now."

Natalie didn't need to be told when they reached the clearing off Pemaquid Road. Even after all these years, her senses revolted against the smell of moldering pine needles. By the glow of the flashlight, they stopped beneath the tree where Teddy had once read *My Brother Sam Is Dead.*

Delia turned on Jason. "Why are you doing this?"

Jason shrugged, his gaze roving. "We got to finish it, don't we? Wrap it up in a bow. Make it pretty." His pupils were black moons. Lowell was right: He and Grace had done more than just drink tonight.

Teddy spoke, his voice trembling. "You got what you wanted—we're scared, all right? Now let us go."

"Can't do that. Don't blame us. Blame your cousin." He shook his head. "Shouldn't've come back, Miss Nat-a-lie. Everybody was happier before you did."

He walked a few feet away, speaking up into the canopy of leaves overhead.

"What did I say that day, when we came up on you two hiding out here?"

He walked over and played the rifle under Teddy's chin, watching as he tried to pull back. "You got a big mouth. Bet I could fit this right in there—"

"Don't touch him!" Natalie lunged for Jason. Grace locked her arms behind her. Natalie thrashed in her grip, not caring that her shoulders felt like they were being wrenched from their sockets. "Get off me!"

"Yeah! Perfect!" Jason laughed. "That's almost exactly right. All we need now is Peter to laugh like an idiot."

"You're trashing Peter?" Lowell sounded hoarse. "That kid thought you were God. All he wanted was to be like you. He ask you to help him while he was lying there bleeding, Jase? He beg you?"

Delia reached for Lowell, but he kept on.

"You let my life get shit-canned right along with yours. The least you can do is tell me why."

Jason looked at him, mouth slightly ajar, eyes hooded. Then he turned to Grace. "I want them on their knees. Like we talked about."

Grace pushed Natalie down, then the others.

Delia swore and started crying, and Teddy bent his head close to hers, squeezing his eyes shut.

When Grace got to Lowell, he pulled away from her. "No."

"Lowell, just *do* it!" Teddy said.

"You're gonna have to shoot me, Grace. You really want to do that for him?" He pointed to Jason. "Huh? Kill somebody? He's laughing at you."

Lowell put his hands up, stepping away. "I'm taking these guys and we're leaving. It ends here."

"You're right," Grace said. "It does." She fired.

Everyone screamed. The shot was still echoing as Natalie crawled across the ground, reaching out to Lowell where he crouched, shielding his head. He squeezed her hand back: *I'm okay.*

"Everybody understand how it's gonna be now?" Grace's roar was huge, bigger than the gunshot. The bullet had gone into the ground inches from where Lowell had stood.

"Everybody see what's happening here? Nobody's screwing with me tonight."

Natalie looked up at Jason. The expression on his face terrified her more than anything that had happened so far.

Jason stood there staring at his girlfriend like she was a stranger, like she'd startled him out of his drugged bravado. His rifle sagged nearly down to the dirt. "Whooooaaa, killer." He gave a splintery chuckle. "We're having fun here. Remember."

"Don't call me that," Grace whispered.

"Babe. Chill, okay? I got this."

Grace paid him no mind, eyes unfocused as they drifted over Natalie's face. "Why didn't you tell?" She sounded like a child, faint and querulous.

"Grace." Jason shifted. "Don't go too far, now. Listen to me."

Her shoulders were hunched, muscles coiled. She reached down and grabbed the front of Natalie's shirt. "Why didn't you tell?"

In the ringing, paralyzed moment that followed, Natalie managed to say, "What?"

"You saw. I know you did." Grace didn't let go as Natalie straightened up. "Christ, I saw you. Why didn't you ever tell?"

Everyone was staring at them.

"What's she talking about?" Lowell said.

The words were spilling out of Grace now. "You ran away

through the trees. I followed you—I found your stupid barrette on the ground. But you acted like you didn't know. How come?" She shook her head slowly. "I waited and waited. When you came back, I was so sure you'd talk. But you didn't."

Memories: trees flying by, crawling on her belly through the bushes, the sight of Peter's dirty white Adidas passing by on the far side of the gully.

"No. I didn't see anything."

Grace's chin shook. "Quit lying." She pointed at the others. "Tell them. You *know*. Peter wouldn't *stop*. He kept grabbing at the gun. You know how he used to be. You'd say no, and he'd keep on working on you until you gave in. Like a little kid." She croaked, somewhere between a sob and a cry. "I told him no because he'd never shot before. I'd gone deer-hunting once, at least."

She opened her hands around the Browning, helplessly. "I told him he couldn't hold it. He grabbed my arm and I pulled away from him and—I didn't even know the safety wasn't on. I thought you'd put it *on*, Jase!" she screamed, making him flinch.

Lowell squeezed his eyes shut.

"Peter fell down and blood came through his shirt so fast and he acted like he was choking, or drowning, or something, and *he*"— she pointed at Jason with the Browning and he stepped back—"he came up after he heard the shot and Peter was lying there and I was saying, We got to get help, we got to get help—and he said we gotta get out of here because the police will come and nobody will think it was an accident and you'll get in trouble—and I just grabbed the gun and we ran—"

"Shut your mouth!" Jason's eyes were wide. "Are you crazy?"

"Hid the gun in the woods behind my gramma's place. Wrapped it in plastic and buried it until it was safe to dig it up." Grace's eyes were streaming. "You get my presents, Natalie? You get the things I left for you?"

"Yes."

"I remembered, about the secret place. Peter told me one time. Said you guys used to leave messages in there. We were going to leave something gross for you guys to find, prank you . . . never got the chance."

"Grace." Natalie could barely control her voice. "I did not see you. I was down too low. All I saw were bushes. I heard Peter talking to somebody and then the shot. I couldn't even remember that much until this summer. I got up and ran away. I never saw you."

Grace tilted her head, eyes bleary. In time, understanding dawned. Something in her expression twisted. She didn't turn to Jason as she addressed him. "You said you did that time in lockup for me. Because of me."

"I did, babe."

"All the things I did . . . because you said so. Because you were the one who really knew. Thought I owed you." She turned her head. "My own mom doesn't want me in her house anymore because of you."

"Now, Gracie—you can't hang that on me. You girls had problems way before—"

"You were never gonna shoot them." Grace gave her shouting laugh. "You talk real big, like a real killer, but you were never gonna do it. You'd play with them a while, and then you'd let them go. Think I didn't know that?" He stared back, unmanned. "Think I didn't know I was gonna have to do all the hard work? All the dirty work?"

Jason hesitated, wavering, five pairs of eyes fixed on him. He pointed toward the woods.

"You know, I'm about ready to walk outta here, Grace. Leave you on your own, see how you do then. You've never been without me *once*. Think you can handle it? Everybody here knows what you did now. Shot your mouth off and spoiled everything for yourself, didn't you?"

He started edging away, shouldering his rifle, expression tight and watchful.

"Forget it. I'm walking."

Grace's upper lip twitched. She said, "Babe, don't." Her voice was small and without fear. Her eyes were like the ocean, shifting and wild. She put her arm out and shot him as a reflex.

The night shattered. Everyone ran. There wasn't time to grab anyone's hand, to make sure Teddy or Delia were on their feet, to see which way Lowell was going. The gun was still firing, Grace was still shooting.

Natalie plunged through the dark woods, hearing the others crashing off through the bushes, screaming. Adrenaline pulsed through her, along with the dream mantra: *Almost time, almost time, almost time.* If she could clear the trees, if she could get to the road, it might be okay, she might make it.

Grace was bathed in moonlight, turning unsteadily, the gun pointed at nothing as she squeezed the trigger, as she fired again, again, again . . .

In the deafening explosion, something parted the air next to Natalie's head. The next bullet took her down.

CHAPTER 33

Natalie stood alone on a road.

"Hello?" Her voice was muffled. Her heartbeat was amplified in her ears.

It was still nighttime, woods on all sides. She had no memory of how she'd gotten here. Dreamy unease spread through her. She searched for the moon. She couldn't find it. There was only a smooth, onyx sky above.

"Where are you guys?" Her voice echoed out, out.

If she tried, she could recall everyone running in different directions, running from something—*what?*—like kids splitting off for a game of hide-and-seek. But whatever this strange state was, she seemed to be in it alone.

Come home, darning needle.

She began walking, slowly becoming aware that she was on Morning Glory Lane. The road was sleeping except for the occasional pair of glowing eyes moving through the woods, a soft *chirrup* from the undergrowth. Nocturnal animals, highly aware of her presence.

She reached the house and found it drenched in splendor. Every window was aglow. Winter light poured from the panes. Natalie felt the rightness of it all now.

She passed through the brambles like a wraith, drawn to the open front door.

We wait for you.

Snow fell from the ceiling, coating her shoulders and hair as she drifted down the hallway into the kitchen. The dream door she had drawn on the wall was open, revealing a square of blinding blue light.

A thread of light separated itself and moved across the air toward her. Natalie watched, paralyzed. With a tugging sensation, the three spirit lights rose from her body. Pieces of souls, returning home.

The spirit lights formed a single globe and joined with the glowing thread, fusing in a flash of light that consumed Natalie entirely. She was lifted up and into the blinding horizon beyond the doorway. She knew no more.

CHAPTER 34

A clock chimed a four-note melody, followed by three reverberating *bongs* tolling the hour. Natalie sat, head in hands, awakening.

There was a harsh wind outside, alternately whistling and moaning away, the ticking of the clock, and a rotten smell. Natalie looked around.

She was crouched on the floor against a wooden counter. To her left sat a cast-iron cookstove with GLENWOOD C stamped on the oven door. A copper kettle sat on the range, burbling away like one gone comfortably mad. There were knitted oven mitts, and tins on the stove shelf labeled FLOUR, COFFEE, and TEA.

She stood. Her nostrils filled with that overripe smell again.

Dishes were everywhere. They covered the countertops and filled the sink, china stacked in piles, teacups upended on saucers. Everything was crusty with smears of moldering food.

Snow. They should be filled with snow. *Oh God, don't let it be don't let it be—*

A 180-degree-turn brought her back to the door, which had been behind her all along: Six panes of rippled glass reflected the kitchen and her own thunderstruck expression.

Natalie muffled her scream too late. She seized a paring knife from the counter and dropped back into the corner.

She remembered light. A sensation of weightlessness, of being drawn forward against her will. Then nothing, until the chiming of the clock.

Natalie grabbed her own flesh and twisted, trying to wake herself up. It hurt.

"What did you do?" she hissed to the girls. "What did you *do?*"

The temptation of checking out was irresistible, of hiding in her mind until the storm passed. She hid her face in her folded arms.

Don't you dare, an internal voice spoke. *Snap out of it.*

Natalie sniffled, still not raising her head.

Listen. Really listen. What do you hear?

She strained for what lay beneath the babbling kettle and the wind. No footsteps, no movement.

Get your bearings. You know this place. In your heart, you know it better than almost anyone.

Natalie held the knife in front of her as she crossed the kitchen, her gaze jumping to the doorway every few seconds. She went to a window and stared out at a winter afternoon. The sky was clouded, considering more snow. Chickadees and blue jays hopped around on the shoveled driveway.

The big black car is gone. He isn't home.

Nothing but fields, miles of them, crosshatched with fence lines tilting in snowdrifts.

"No," she whispered, striking her fist against glass, willing this dream-image to shatter.

Maybe this shouldn't be possible. But you can see it, you can feel it, so it's real. He'll find you. It's what he does. All he knows how to do is satisfy his hungers, and stay alive.

She whimpered, but she was already moving toward the hallway door.

The girls brought you here for a reason, darning needle.

The corridor seemed endless in her terror, slanting and telescopic. At the end, the foyer was barely recognizable. Lace curtains flanked the front door. The fanlight projected a dappled crown of daylight onto the floor. The grandfather clock stood against the hallway wall, and Natalie looked up at it in awe. There was a moving mechanism in the face which rotated a celestial illustration with the passing hours. Now, the image was halfway between sun and moon.

Get moving. Think.

Edith.

If this was December 1948, then Edith Soucy was in the barn right now, dying or dead. It might not be too late.

Natalie lunged for the front door, and then pulled her hand back from the cold knob. Right. Winter.

She ran upstairs and let herself into Raisa's bedroom. The air was stagnant, choked with dust. Apparently Vsevolod wasn't a big believer in housekeeping. Why should he be? This was only a den, a place to rest and recoup between hunts. Through the window, the slope of a high barn roof was visible, hung with icicles as thick as her arm.

She searched in the closet for something warm to wear over her T-shirt and shorts, finding a pair of woolen pants to squeeze into and a sweater. She slipped the knife into her hip pocket.

Downstairs, she went to the overloaded hall tree, draped with coats and hats. She dug into the pockets of his tartan-flannel coat. It smelled of him—that was the most incapacitating thing—and she held her breath, touching loose change, a matchbook, and finally, the padlock key.

She went through the door with the six panes into a summer kitchen. It was crowded with old junk, probably left by the farm family who'd owned the place before: Humpty Dumpty potato chip tins, piles of yellowed newspapers dating back to the 1920s.

The door at the end opened into Vsevolod's workshop. A sign leaned against the wall: GEORGE DAWES, MASTER CARPENTER. CUSTOM-BUILT FURNITURE—INQUIRE WITHIN.

She ran. It was as if she could hear the hallway clock inside of her, keeping time.

The final door of the winter passage let out onto the haymow of the barn, the floor intact, the air still smelling of livestock. As Natalie went through, a sound from outside made her turn.

In all that winter silence, a car engine purred, drawing closer.

It might not be.

Her muscles tightened as she faced the window, already shaking her head at her own reassurances, fumbling for the knife. Not a car had passed since she'd been here.

It was Vsevolod. Coming home.

CHAPTER 35

The Dodge sedan coupe, all chrome and black enamel, pulled into the dooryard. There was very little daylight left now. Vsevolod gathered his things and climbed out into the frigid air, hefting two crates of groceries in his arms.

Natalie's breath caught.

He was far larger in person, broad through the shoulders and chest, dressed in a charcoal car coat and fedora. There was very little daylight left now.

He didn't know she was here, *couldn't* know.

Once Natalie had seen him open the front door, she slipped out the rear door of the barn. The cold hit her and she gasped, tucking her hands into her armpits; it didn't help that these pants left about three inches of ankle exposed. She ran, skidding the last few feet down to the basement door.

Natalie pressed her ear to the door. What if her only response was a heavy, telling silence?

"Edith? Can you hear me?"

No answer.

Natalie bit her lip as she fumbled with the padlock. "Edith, I'm here to help you. Please say something if you can."

A scrabbling sound. Edith's fingertips, scratching on the other side.

Natalie rested her forehead against the door for a second, fighting tears. "Hold on."

When she opened the door, Edith fell out in a cloud of kerosene fumes, still wrapped in the canvas tarpaulin, and Natalie experienced another moment of awe—this was actually happening.

Natalie dragged her farther out into the fresh air, unwilling to look back at the blackness where Irene's corpse lay. Edith stuffed clumps of snow into her mouth. She sat up, swallowing, barely conscious but still focusing bloodshot eyes on Natalie.

"I didn't know if you were real," Edith slurred.

"*Shhh*. He's right inside the house. Come on."

Natalie saw the girl's hands. Some of her fingers were black. Frostbite. Natalie cursed.

Edith dropped back on one elbow, eyelids fluttering. "Cold." She drew her head toward the crook of her arm.

"Wake *up*. We have to get inside the barn." Natalie shook Edith's shoulder, patted her cheeks with snow; obviously, she had to get mean. "Edith, snap out of it! Get on your feet and *move*! You want to die out here?"

Edith could barely walk. Once they were inside the barn proper, Natalie found a mound of moldy hay in the corner of one stall and dug a hole, pushing Edith down into it.

"Hide in there, okay?"

Edith's eyes brightened a little and the stubborn set returned to her mouth; if she'd had her way, she probably would've slugged Natalie right there. "You're leaving?"

"Somebody's got to get help. You can't run. You'd just slow me down."

There was an old horse blanket folded over the stall door, and Natalie spread it out on Edith. Under a layer of hay, she'd be completely hidden from sight.

When Edith spoke next, she sounded drowsy. "What're you gonna do?"

Natalie thought. How far did this world go? Did the actual 1948 town of Bernier exist out there? Would she find the sardine cannery running, the dock churning with life?

"It'll be dark soon. We've got to take his car."

She placed handfuls of hay over Edith, watching her twitch as she sank back into a semiconscious state.

"I'll be back as soon as I can. Keep still until I come for you, okay?"

No response. The girl had passed out.

The keys might be in the car. Suddenly, Natalie would've given anything to have Teddy here, walking these unwilling steps with her into the cold. For a moment, memory flickered—*a gunshot?*—and then went out.

It was flurrying in the twilight now. She lifted her gaze to the barn's roof peak and felt a dizzying sensation of vertigo; it seemed to go up and up forever. Her eyes followed the connected buildings back to the main house and saw a lamp glowing in a second-story bedroom window.

She skirted the front of the house, praying he wouldn't part the curtains at that moment and spot her. People did leave their keys in their cars sometimes, didn't they? Especially if they lived way out in the country . . .

Natalie dove into the snow behind the car, gasping, unaware that she'd begun to cry. She eased the passenger-side door open. The interior of the coupe was darkly oiled, fragrant. She stretched across the bench seat, leather squeaking beneath her.

The ignition was empty. Natalie tried the glove box, then the visors. The ashtray held nothing but scrunched cigarette butts. She jammed her hand under the seat, along the cushion, places where keys would never be. "Come on, *please*." Blinded by tears, she covered her face.

You need to keep moving. That voice was back. *If the keys are in the house, you'll just have to go get them.*

"No. I can't."

You must want to die here, then. Edith, too.

Natalie cursed and fled.

Cutting through the workshop and summer kitchen was excruciating. Every step felt loaded, threatening a creaky board or a stumble. If only she could hide until he went to bed. If only it wasn't a matter of time before Edith's strength gave out. Natalie gripped her knife, ready to slash. Outside, it was now snowing heavily.

She ducked against the summer kitchen door and peered into the house through the glass panes. Lamps were burning inside and the grocery cartons sat empty on the table. She didn't see the car keys. *Oh God, I cannot do this.* Yet she was doing it. To her own horror, she was already in the kitchen.

Her flesh crawled. She was shaking in a way she'd only read about in books. She inched forward, hearing music from another room. She bit her fist. No car keys in sight. Maybe they were in his coat pocket. Or, worse, his pants pocket. No choice but to go to the hall tree and check the charcoal coat, praying he stayed occupied.

The hallway stretched as long as a Pullman car. There was a faint creak as he shifted his weight on the parlor floorboards, only about twenty feet away from where she stood. Natalie touched the coat as if it might burn her. A canned voice crowed, "Yeah, *man*," some swing orchestra tripping the light fantastic on the turntable. The *keys*. She felt the pear shape of the smallest *matryoshka* doll in her fingers.

A shrill chime split the air, and Natalie gasped, turning, realizing too late that it was only the clock breaking into its hourly song. Her arm brushed the overloaded coats. As if in slow motion, they spilled across the bench and onto the floor with a clatter of buttons and clasps.

Natalie shrank back. Impossible to tell amid the din of the music and the clock, but she knew he'd heard her. She knew he was standing quite still in the parlor right now, head cocked.

Heavy footsteps started in her direction. She bolted. Behind her, the picture on the clock face stood at full moon.

Natalie rushed back through the summer kitchen and would've blown through the workshop, too, if she hadn't remembered Edith. She couldn't lead him to her.

She ran to the end of the room, threw open the door to the barn, and then ran back and hid behind the workshop door. She could already hear heavy footsteps in the summer kitchen. Her chest hurt; she couldn't breathe. She closed her eyes, imagining a bear, a Kodiak, its wet, fist-size nose twitching, exploring the air. The bear only wanted to find her, that's all. Only wanted to fit its jaws around her skull and crush, crush, crush . . .

Natalie bit her lips together, blood thundering in her ears.

Please let him see the open door and think I ran through to the back fields. Let him look for me while I reach the car. Please, Raisa, Irene, somebody—help.

She heard the creak of his weight in the doorway. Vsevolod was using the stillness, probably studying the gaping doorway across the workshop. Time stretched on. Then he hit the lights.

Bulbs strung along the beams burst into life. The last of Natalie's breath wheezed between her lips.

Vsevolod stepped through the doorway and immediately saw Natalie out of the corner of his eye. He didn't whip around to face her; he turned his head slowly as if he didn't trust his own senses, finding her standing there against the wall, staring back.

Neither of them spoke. Vsevolod's eyes were interested and his mouth crooked with a hint of puzzled amusement. He'd slicked the front of his hair with oil; the back waved and curled around the nape of his neck. He wore dark trousers, a collared shirt beneath a sweater. He'd been eating pineapple chunks and still held the can; now he remembered it and set it on the workbench, never looking away from her.

"Well," he said, and she flinched at the deep, all-too-familiar sound of his voice, "this is a fine how-do-you-do." He spoke teasingly, as if aware that someone offstage was playing a joke on him. "And who are we?"

A drop of sweat coursed down her temple. When she said nothing, he stepped forward.

She slid back along the wall.

"Do you want to tell me what you're doing in my house?" This time he spoke with exaggerated slowness, as if she might be partially deaf or touched in the head.

Think of something, any stupid lie. Words slipped through her grasp. Surely he'd taken in her dark hair and heavy build; she wasn't his type. He might let her go. Her left hand squeezed around the knife, hidden behind her. The car keys were in her back pocket.

"I'm lost," a small, quiet voice said, and it took her a moment to recognize it as her own.

Vsevolod continued to stare. The minute details of his person were overwhelming: the missing top button of his sweater, the light reflecting in his eyes.

"I thought this was someone else's house." Her voice trembled and he smiled.

"Nobody lives out here but me."

He moved closer and enjoyed seeing her recoil, ducking into a corner that was no protection at all. He couldn't know why she was so afraid already, only that he was the reason. The smile widened into a grin, showing teeth yellowed with nicotine.

"Now, are you sure it wasn't me you were looking for?"

She saw the change in him as he finally recognized what she wore.

The smile dropped. His dark eyes snapped to her face, instantly wild. He grabbed two fistfuls of her sweater and lifted her until she stood on tiptoe. He began shaking her slowly. "We've caught a thief," he whispered, his face in hers as she grimaced against his hot, sweet pineapple breath, "yes, we have. Fox in the henhouse."

"I—" She said the first thing she thought of: "Raisa knows what you did to those girls."

A flux of emotion passed over his face. He faltered.

She threw her knee into his groin. She wasn't exactly on target, but still he grunted and doubled forward, releasing her. She hesitated for a half-second, her arm raised, before driving the knife into him.

She felt the blade sink into his shoulder. He roared and swiped out at her, knocking her sideways. The knife was gone—still *in* him.

Natalie ran through the darkness of the barn, out the rear door into the storm. Snow slanted into her face.

She beat a path toward the milk house. Hiding behind it, she wailed silently into her cupped hands.

It wasn't long before Vsevolod came through the back doorway with one hand to his shoulder checking for blood, his expression savage. He made toward the east side of the barn. Checking on Edith.

Hollow bangs echoed across the fields as he smashed his fist into something again and again, probably the barn door. Natalie rocked until silence fell. His footsteps came back around the house and the door slammed shut.

Could she still reach the car in time? She had the keys. A vision of his arms closing around her was enough to stop her from trying it. Every place he'd touched burned with a livid, unpleasant heat.

Where were the girls in this world? How could they leave her here alone? "What do I *do*?" she cried. "Help me!"

Behind the milk house, there was nothing but an expanse of fields. Beyond that, woods, promising confusion, misdirection, as night fell. It would be suicide in a storm. But somewhere, miles off, there was another farm, wasn't there? The Page Farm.

She would take her chances in the trees.

By the time he came through the back door, she was only a flash of movement disappearing into the wilderness. Hoisting his lantern, he gave chase.

CHAPTER 36

She flew through the woods, giddy with her speed and luck, swatting aside branches, pushing through drifts. He should be right on top of her, but he wasn't. Vsevolod seemed to have blended away into the storm.

Soon, the darkness thickened. She couldn't judge proportion anymore. Wind buffeted her with endless grainy curtains of snow. She fell and fell.

She wasn't escaping. Vsevolod was tracking her from a distance, following the sounds of her crashing through the snow like a wounded deer. Even with his limp, he'd catch her.

Run, run, until you pray for release. Then you'll welcome my strangler's embrace, you'll all but beg me for it—

"No!" She sprawled, chafing her palms and chin on the icy crust. Moaning, she moved deeper into the labyrinth.

Full night pressed down on her. She wove through a bramble patch she couldn't see. By the end, she was calling out for Mom and Dad, Teddy, Lowell. She remembered with dull shock that none of them existed here.

She turned, raising her fists. "Do something!" Nothing answered but the wind. "*Come on and do something!*" She screamed threats and curses until her voice cracked. Her blind eyes played tricks on her, producing flashes in the darkness, amorphous shapes. She fled.

The snow was deeper now, above her knees in places. Natalie's hair was tangled with sticks and brambles, and her skin, wind-burned scarlet. Instinct assured her that Vsevolod was still close. She'd stolen his prize. As far as he knew, Edith had reached help by now, and the police were on their way. Irrationally, madly, he'd hunt Natalie to the end.

Without warning, the ground dropped away. Natalie pinwheeled down a slope and hit bottom hard. After a stunned moment, she stood—something crunched—and she fell through ice.

Water surged around her. Huffing, she flailed, fragments break-ing off in her hands as she tried to grab hold. December ice, thin as candied glass.

Her toes scraped bottom. She could touch. Grinding her toes into the silt, Natalie pushed forward, grunting, finding the embank-ment little more than an arm's length away.

Elbow by knee, she crawled out of the stream. She was shud-dering violently. An option materialized—slipping back into the water, sinking, letting go—but, defeated, she simply lay there.

This is what Edith felt when she was locked under the barn, forc-ing herself to walk in circles. Natalie began coughing. *Her own time running out.*

The wind rose. She lifted her head . . . and for a moment, something flickered in the storm. The eyes of an animal? Maybe she'd imagined it, seeing fireflies in a snowstorm. She stood, swaying.

There *was* a light. A flame hovered several yards away, casting shadows across the snow. She went to it, her body and mind at the end of their resistance.

A lantern hung from a branch, swinging gently as she watched in an exhausted stupor. *A trap.* She couldn't rouse, couldn't run. *He's baiting you; you swallowed the hook—*

Footsteps crashed toward her. The rough shape of him broke the lantern's glow, hands outstretched. Two polished bronze discs for eyes, a quicksilver flash of teeth below. He was grinning. In the end, her own animal scream broke her paralysis and let her run.

He struck a double-fisted blow between her shoulder blades. She went down.

He wrenched her over and straddled her. She couldn't kick, could barely move. The struggle was wordless, grunts and screams. Natalie punched him until he cuffed her wrists in one hand and watched her writhe for a while, his expression one of softness and distance, his cologne scent choking her. Then his hands found her throat and bore down.

Air stopped. She clawed his face, felt sandpaper stubble, the slickness of his teeth as he mockingly snapped at her and laughed.

A gray tide rose, dulling everything, even the pain, but she registered a stick or rock jabbing her backside—*poke, poke*—insistently. An image of the tiny *matryoshka* doll drifted before her, a piece of string noosed around its neck. *Back pocket.* She worked one hand down. His nose was touching hers. The keys were in her hand now, between thumb and forefinger. She stabbed at his face. He didn't have time to recoil before she struck something very tender.

His sound of pain was horrible. Natalie sucked air as she

wriggled between his legs, crawled across the snow, her vision tilting like a funhouse tunnel. Trees—the lantern hanging—

Vsevolod wailed something in half-English, half-Russian, and then he was crawling up her. She bit his hand and lurched to her feet. The lantern. She ripped it down and swung it out in a wide arc.

Vsevolod's great, cold hands were inches away, his eyes metallic discs again in the light. The lantern struck his temple like a mallet. He dropped.

"Come on!" she rasped, ready to hit him again. He didn't move. She backed away, coughing, spitting. "Come on, dammit!"

There was blood on his teeth, much more at his temple. Strange, seeing him at rest, eyelids fluttering. She'd cut him beneath his left eye and across his cheekbone and lips with the car keys. He'd prepared well for the stalk through the woods, wearing his heavy coat with a scarf knotted into the collar and a watch cap. He groaned softly, gloved fingers working the snow, and then he went still. Maybe died. She didn't know. She only wanted to run.

Natalie raised the lantern and did just that.

It snowed harder. Adrenaline kept her going another fifteen minutes, but eventually her limbs grew leaden. She was spent. Her thoughts were muddled, trying to reason out which way to go. Free of Vsevolod or pursued by him, she was still lost in these woods. The blizzard was worsening. She saw nothing but white even when she closed her eyes. A poem she'd read in English class returned to her, whispering serenely, *And miles to go before I sleep, And miles to go before I sleep.*

Natalie fell. No internal voice told her to soldier on; perhaps it had gone to sleep, too. The lantern landed in the snow but the wick continued to burn. There was almost no oil left.

Small, iridescent eyes observed her from the edge of the lantern's reach. It was a cat. She watched in fuzzy bemusement as it backed away and slipped through the trees. Perhaps it was never really there at all.

She believed she was dead, interred under feet of warm soil. What sort of flowers would grow from her? Wild roses? Goldenrod? What would her body look like six months gone, two years, sixty years?

She became aware of a light. She forced her eyes open. It hovered over her in the driving snow.

"—hear me?"

She tried to scream, producing a croaking noise through the swollen tissues of her throat.

"Oh, Lordy. You hold on, dear. Hold right onto me."

Hands went under her arms. She would've fought if she'd had the strength. This voice wasn't his, but somehow it would *always* be him, and it would always be these woods, a never-ending chase through blinding snow. Vsevolod around every tree, reaching for her.

She fainted.

CHAPTER 37

When Natalie awoke, she was dry. She simply lay there, eyes closed, savoring it. She rolled onto her side, smelling a woodstove fire burning nearby.

She was in the house again. The copper kettle sang and the dishes were spread willy-nilly and the bear was sniffing her out, room to room, down endless passageways of night.

Natalie lurched forward, gasping at the pain. This kitchen was unfamiliar. Small, with busy wallpaper and the odor of baked beans and bread in the air.

"She's up," said a man's quiet, elderly voice, and Natalie looked at the three people who stood from the kitchen table to face her.

She began to cough, spitting up phlegm and clots of blood. Somebody put a rag to her mouth. Natalie felt her swollen, puffy throat. It hurt to breathe.

"There. You get that nasty stuff up, and you'll feel better."

A warm hand brushed her head and she jerked back; the woman *tsk*ed mildly.

"Look at that. Somebody throttled her. Those are finger marks if I've ever seen them."

Natalie recognized Mrs. Page. She'd drawn a chair over to her cot and held the rag in one hand, her expression unperturbed. Her eyes were brilliant behind horn-rimmed glasses, and she reached back to the table, producing a teacup.

"Take a little sip. Might burn at first, but get it down anyway."

It did burn, mightily, and Natalie spit most of it back up.

The others exchanged looks. There was a tall, horse-faced gentleman with white hair peeking out from beneath his plaid cap—Mr. Page, no doubt. He was dressed in work slacks and a chamois shirt with suspenders. A young man with a beard stood a few feet back. He fiddled with a cloth napkin, turning it over in his hands.

"What's your name, dear? Hmm?" Mrs. Page rubbed her arm soothingly. "Where'd you come from?"

Natalie spoke, her voice wheezing and rough. "He tried to kill me."

"Who?"

She realized no one would know Vsevolod's real name, and searched for his alias. "Dawes. The man who lives on the hill."

Heavy silence fell. Mrs. Page pursed her lips and sat back, exhaling.

"Well, there." She looked at her husband significantly, who studied his boots. "You better tell us all about it."

Natalie tried to sit up again. "He's got two more girls in the barn. One's still alive. Her name's Edith Soucy, and she's hurt. Worse than me. She needs help right away, or else she—"

She broke off coughing.

"Holy Jesus," the young man breathed, and Mr. Page frowned at him.

Mrs. Page lifted the bottom of the teacup, urging Natalie to drink some more.

"Well, you're with friends now. My name's Elizabeth Page, and that's my husband Owen, and our youngest son, Jim. You're in our kitchen and nobody's going to lay a finger on you." She sighed. "It was a providence Owen spotted you in this storm."

"Looked out the barn window," Owen said slowly, shaking his head. "Don't know why. Don't make a habit of looking out the window when I'm tending the cows, I can tell you, but tonight I did. And there you were, in the woods."

"I was trying to get here." Sleep was threatening again, heavy and irresistible. "What is this?" she said, looking down at the teacup, now nearly empty.

"Hot toddy. Good for the chills." Mrs. Page cleared her throat. "So George Dawes is the one who put his hands on you?" When Natalie nodded: "He chased you through all them woods?" Another nod. Mrs. Page smoothed the top of the blankets. "You from town? I don't know your face, is all."

"Somebody's got to get up there. I don't think he'll go back to the farm. I think I killed him, in the woods."

Natalie was barely aware of the change that came over their faces, of Mrs. Page's eyes widening behind the lenses of her spectacles.

"Somebody's got to help Edith, or she'll die."

Owen said, "Jim, get on the horn to the sheriff and Doc Brower." His son started toward the hall. "I'll get the truck warmed up."

"Owen Page!" Mrs. Page half-stood. "You taken a peek outside lately?"

"If there's somebody up there hurt, I can get there a lot faster than the law or Doc."

"And suppose Dawes shows up? He's a big son of a buck, and if he's been carrying on like she says—"

"I'll bring Jim and my Winchester. That suit you?"

Natalie broke in. "Edith's in the last stall, under some hay."

She dropped back against the pillow, watching the way the light fixture overhead doubled in her blurring vision.

"Irene's under the barn. I came too late for her." She began to cry, picturing Irene's sweet, round face the night of the Halloween dance. "I'm so sorry." She cried harder.

Mrs. Page rubbed her back, talking quietly to the men. "Dress warm, both of you, and for God's sake, take care of yourselves. If you see any sign of that fella, put a bullet in him. If even half of this is true, nobody will fault you for it."

Eventually, there came the sound of the door shutting, the whisper of wind cut off snugly. Mrs. Page sat close, smelling of flowery talc.

"Fix you another toddy, that's what I'll do. Rest now. Sleep's what you need." She made a frustrated hissing sound. "Go on, don't be a pest."

An orange tiger cat wound around the legs of the cot. It gazed up at Natalie, its eyes round as dimes. "Is that your cat?" she asked faintly.

"You might say. He sort of chose us." Mrs. Page gave it a perfunctory pat on the head before depositing it on the warm hearth.

"He's a roamer, all right. Comes and goes as he pleases. He was out in the storm till just a minute ago, fool thing."

It was undeniably Raisa's cat, fully grown now and apparently none the worse for his drop from a second-story window. Nine lives. As if from far away, Natalie heard Mrs. Page whisper again, wonderingly, "Where in the world did you come from, girl?"

Natalie slept.

When she awoke, the room was dim. The fire had been allowed to burn down to ashes. The cat was gone. Feeling more alert, Natalie sat up, looking around the room which had been so full of the sounds and smells of life.

"Mrs. Page?" Her voice had a hollow note, as if she'd called into a deep stone well. The pale light filtering through the windows had no particular quality of day or evening, but as she watched, frost began crackling across the glass, sill to sill, quilting a patchwork of ice.

Across the room, the front door opened slowly, as if pushed by a breeze. Light filled the entryway. In it, three globules chased each other in secret ghosts' games. Natalie felt no fear as they came for her.

There was faint laughter in the light. It wove around her. Natalie closed her eyes and returned to oblivion.

CHAPTER 38

The house waited in fields of brambles.

Natalie walked up the path to the front door. The sun was bright and she propped her hand above her eyes.

Raisa sat on the step, smiling, wearing one of her housedresses with a full apron over it. The sun had bronzed her forehead and cheekbones, and her dark eyes were squinted against the light.

The day stuttered like a bad film reel, spilling the scene sideways, and Natalie blinked, disconcerted as it righted itself. A question came to her: "Did I fix things?"

Raisa twined her fingers together, pulled them apart. "You're a good girl. You tried to mend it."

Someone stood in the far field, watching them. It was Irene in her party dress, her hair blowing loosely around her shoulders. She looked back at Natalie, not quite smiling but with warmth in her expression. "But I didn't help her," Natalie said. "Or you. You're both still . . ."

"We're ready for a long sleep." Raisa's gaze was bottomless. "Irene and me. Edith's the one who wants to keep going. That's all she's ever wanted." She studied her hands. "You ought to be getting home now."

Natalie looked at the field, where Irene waited. Beyond her, the whip-poor-will called and called. It sounded very close.

The scene stuttered again, and then Raisa and Irene were together in the field, running and laughing, circling each other in a game of their own creation. The bird called once more, triumphantly.

The girls waved good-bye, far away.

The hands of time let Natalie go.

Somewhere in the dissonance of sound and sensation, Natalie screamed as the memories washed back over her. She was on a platform shooting down a corridor of alabaster, people clinging to all sides, jabbering, repeating her name. Her eyes rolled back in her head.

Natalie saw someone reaching out to cup her face.

"Hon." Mom's eyes were wide and bloodshot as she stood over the bed. "Natalie, relax. You're going to be okay. You're in the hospital. Do you hear me?"

Someone unfolded himself from the chair in the corner, tall and broad-shouldered, raising his hands up from his sides. Natalie let out a thin scream, covering her face.

"What in the world?" Dad, who'd been half-asleep in the chair while *Wheel of Fortune* contestants exuded muted fervor on the TV screen, stopped where he was. "Deb, you better press that button now."

Natalie had a gauze bandage on the left side of her head. A patch of her hair had been shaved, the doctor told her, so that they could stitch up the gash left by the bullet that had grazed her.

The doctor explained her injuries. Her head wound had resulted in a subdural hematoma and a period of unconsciousness lasting about three hours. He asked her about her injured throat, frowning as he reexamined her bruises.

"You don't remember anyone choking you, grabbing you?"

She said no.

Later, he let her parents back into the room.

"Remember me?" Dad gave a nervous chuckle as he stopped several feet from the end of the bed.

"I'm so sorry, Dad." She burst into tears.

Her parents held her hands. When Natalie finally got herself under control, she sniffed, looking up at them. "Where is everyone? Teddy, Lowell, Delia? Are they okay?"

"Everybody's fine." Mom looked haggard, as if this one day had aged her a year. "Delia flagged down a car and got some help. Lowell stayed with you until the ambulance came." She frowned a little, as if his name was bitter on her tongue and would take some getting used to. "I'm told he pressed his shirt against your wound, slowed the bleeding. We might not have you here with us if he hadn't. Jason was shot too; Teddy stayed with him, kept him conscious. He was coughing up a lot of blood."

"What about Grace?" Natalie took a deep, unsteady breath.

Mom was some time in answering. "Grace shot until the bullets were gone. We're lucky she didn't kill all of you. Apparently she just sat there until the police came. She won't speak to anyone.

Jason's here now, under guard. The bullet collapsed his right lung. He came through surgery okay, and they think he'll recover."

Dad rubbed his face. "Jesus. Will this ever end?"

Natalie closed her eyes, drifting in exhaustion. "After the bullet hit me, I woke up on the other side of town." She laughed a little, her voice scratchy and weak. "And the house was full of snow." She fought to keep her eyes open. "I really need to see Teddy. Will you bring him?"

Her parents exchanged worried looks. "In the morning. Rest now."

Delia called later.

"Teddy put himself between me and a gun." She laughed shakily. "I can't stop thinking about that. What if she'd shot him? You think . . . he really would've stood there and taken a bullet for me?"

"Most likely, yeah."

"*Why?*"

"He's just like that. There when you need him." Natalie tugged at a loose thread on her hospital gown. "He's something special."

Natalie spent the night under observation. The nurse who came in to wake her every few hours grew increasingly dismayed to find that she was never asleep.

"You should really try to rest," she said, taking Natalie's pulse and studying her pale, drawn expression.

Natalie rolled onto her side. Her head hurt. Her throat ached.

Think about nothing, she told herself, nothing at all; then you can't be afraid of moving branches outside the window, the whisper of crepe-soled footsteps in the hall, a grinning beast in hospital garb with eyes of brass and blood in his teeth, leaning over the bed—*We've caught a thief, yes we have . . . fox in the henhouse*—

The next morning, the rest of the family arrived. Cilla sobbed as she hugged Natalie.

"I am so sorry. I never dreamed—I should've driven you straight home myself, not wasted a second—"

Natalie wiped her aunt's tears with her thumb. "You couldn't have known how far gone Grace and Jason were. Nobody did."

Teddy was hollow-eyed, lingering toward the back of the group even as his gaze locked with Natalie's. She rose up from her pillows, hardly noticing as the conversation trickled to a stop.

"Can I talk to Teddy alone?" she said. The baffled silence continued. "Please?"

Cilla was the first to speak. "Of course. We'll be right outside." She squeezed her son's shoulder as she passed.

Teddy took a seat. His cheekbone had bruised to a deep shade of plum, and he actually appeared to have lost weight. When had she last seen him, twelve hours ago? A lifetime.

"Thought you were a goner," Teddy said. "There was so much blood."

"I heard you had the honor of keeping Jason alive." She watched as he rolled his eyes and glanced away. "You know he wouldn't have done the same for you." Natalie looked at him for a long moment, her eyes filling. "I went back, Teddy. I was there."

He didn't react.

"The girls took me. In that moment, when the bullet hit me"—her eyes stung with tears as she gestured to her bandage—"I could've died. But the girls snatched me up, like they'd always planned to. I did what they wanted, so they let me come home."

Teddy was silent. "You were in 1948?" He leaned forward. "Tell me."

She hesitated in places, cried in others. When she was done, he said, "You think it really happened? You fixed things?"

"The girls are gone. I can feel it." She touched her chest. "There's a hollow place inside me now. I can't think of a better way to describe it. I never knew they were there, but now that they're gone . . ."

"So . . . that means Edith must've made it. If the Pages got her help in time."

There was a knock, and Lowell looked around the curtain. "Oh. Sorry."

"No, no, come in." Natalie sat up.

Teddy got to his feet. "I'll talk to you later."

The boys edged around each other, but at the last second, Lowell said, "Hey." Teddy stopped, facing forward. "Look. I just wanted to say . . . you did really good out there. In the woods. If you hadn't told me to put pressure on her wound, Nat could've died. Jason, too." He put his hand out. "So, thanks."

Teddy looked at his hand for a long moment. When he shook with him, it was fast and hard, over in an instant. Then he was gone.

As Lowell leaned over the bed, she hugged him tightly. He took a seat; his eyes were bloodshot and it looked like he hadn't slept.

"I can't believe what happened. Grace was so messed up. I just never knew. I mean, I knew she had problems, but hell, who doesn't?"

Natalie gave a small shrug. "It sounds like she'd cut herself off from everybody except Jason. And he ground it in, what she'd done. Made everything worse, made her paranoid. I guess as long as she felt like dirt, he could control her." She paused. "Is he really going to be okay?"

"The doctors say he'll be fine after some rehab. Then, back to lockup until they set bail."

"Grace is going away for a long time, huh?"

"Oh, yeah." Lowell took his cap off, shoved his hair back, and clamped the cap down again. "I guess she finally talked, told the cops everything. They understand how it was with Peter now."

"So you believe her? You think it was an accident?"

He nodded. "I've been up most of the night asking myself that. Running through everything I remember about the four of us, the way we were back then. Grace and Peter were buddies. She had no reason to want to hurt him. He was an ass and he could drive you nuts sometimes, but he was one of us. Yeah, I believe her. I think it was a stupid mistake that turned into something a lot worse once Jason got in the middle." He was lost in thought for a moment, and then said, "Cops talk to you yet?"

"The doctor said they'll be sending somebody over."

"There's going to be a trial, you know. Probably not until next year. But we'll need to testify." Lowell frowned, a shadow passing over his face as he straightened up. "Déjà vu all over again, huh. Bet you're wicked glad you came back to your old hometown."

She smiled and held his hand. "In some ways." She ruminated. "I can't believe Grace thought that I was keeping the secret for her. For *two years*. She was so messed up that it must've made sense to her that I would hold the truth over her like Jason, play games. I wish I'd known." She squeezed his hand. "Do me a favor. Don't go anywhere for a while, okay?"

Lowell kissed the back of her hand. "No place I'd rather be."

CHAPTER 39

One Year Later

Natalie parked her '98 Accord in Cilla's driveway and went up the porch steps, knocking once on the screen door before letting herself in.

Teddy was waiting for her in the kitchen, looking over some papers.

"How was the drive?" He craned his neck to see around her as she came in. "So that's the new ride. Very cherry."

"Oh, absolutely. And there's plenty of room in back to carry your bike."

She laughed at his sour expression and sat. They hadn't seen each other since Christmas, but as always, she felt easier when Teddy was around. He'd texted her last week, said he'd found some new articles that she had to see, and maybe it was time for another visit to Bernier.

She picked up the newspaper printouts he was reading. "You kept them all."

"Yeah. I read through them sometimes. You know, to convince myself that it all really happened." He rubbed his eye beneath his glasses. "Sometimes even then I don't believe it."

The top articles were all stories Teddy had run off from microfilm last fall, researching what had come next that winter of 1948. OLD ORCHARD BEACH GIRL ESCAPES KIDNAPPER; CORPSE FOUND UNDER BARN. Owen and Jim Page had found Edith unconscious in the hay, right where Natalie had left her. They'd risked a drive through the worst snowstorm since 1942 to get her into town for help.

GOOD SAMARITAN NEVER CAME BACK, SAYS O.O.B. ABDUCTEE; POLICE SEARCH FOR CLUES. According to Edith and the Page family, another girl in her teens had escaped from George Dawes that night, one who they claimed to have rescued from the snow and spoken with at length. The girl—Natalie—had vanished from the cot in Mrs. Page's kitchen after the older woman left her side, leaving nothing behind but rumpled blankets and unanswered questions.

"Are you sleeping okay these days?" Teddy watched her.

"Not bad."

The dream of the house was gone, replaced by occasional nightmares of running down corridors, of having the life choked from her. She rubbed her throat absently.

"So you said you found something new."

Teddy flipped to the bottom of the pile. "I called the Old Orchard Beach Library a couple weekends ago. Had them search the microfilm."

In 1952, the local paper had run a short human interest story titled SURVIVOR GOES WEST. Edith, something of a local celebrity after her ordeal, was moving on. The gossipy little article reported her plans to move to California in May and look for work in the film industry.

"There's nothing after that," he said. "Who knows what happened to her, where she ended up."

Natalie was silent a moment. "I guess Edith didn't have to be somebody special, or famous, or the mother of a future president or anything. She was just a girl who wouldn't give up on her own life."

It took her back to the woods, the darkness and the snow, the honest belief that she was going to die. She could still feel the weight of the lantern in her hands.

"I hit him so hard, Teddy. I swear to God. He wasn't moving, and there was so much blood. I just—couldn't make myself check to see—"

His voice was firm. "Hurt that bad, he couldn't have gotten far. Not in the middle of a snowstorm. They never found his body, that's all. Lots of times they don't. You know what those woods are like. If you're lucky, some hunter might trip over your bones ten years later."

The kitchen fell quiet, only the sound of the ticking clock, a bird chirping outside.

"Listen, we need to go to the house," he said.

She looked at him sharply.

"Trust me. You need to see this."

Natalie drove them to Morning Glory Lane. She hadn't been back since last July, hadn't been sure she'd ever want to come this way again.

"Here we go." Teddy sat forward. "Look."

The land suddenly opened up, entire fields unfurling where trees had stood a few months earlier. White split-rail fences began shooting by. Natalie sat forward, gazing at the panorama before them.

Belted Galloway cows, black with a white stripe around their middles, were scattered across pasturage on either side of the road, maybe a hundred and fifty head in all.

When they came upon the house in the distance, Natalie didn't hit the brakes. Her foot simply slid off the gas pedal and, after a fashion, the car came shuddering to a stop. She pulled onto the shoulder and they both got out of the car, Natalie holding the edge of her door for support.

"I don't believe this," she breathed. "You didn't tell me."

The house had new owners. It had been painted dark green with white trim, and a copper cow weathervane turned slowly upon the cupola. Work was still being done—it would take more than a year to get the building 100 percent—but people were obviously living here. The barn was in the process of being torn down, and a new prefab outbuilding sat back on the hill to house the cows.

Beneath the mailbox was a sign which read FRESH EGGS—MILK—BUTTER—CREAM FOR SALE. Near the front door, another sign was nailed to the clapboards: LEARY FARM 1770.

Teddy put his hands in his pockets. "I heard somebody had bought the place. I biked out here last month and was totally blown away."

It took Natalie a long time to catch her breath. She fought not to cry with a smile on her face. "It's beautiful."

"Yeah. It is."

Natalie started walking up the driveway.

"What're you doing?" asked Teddy. He caught up with her at the front door. "Are you nuts?" He stared as she rang the bell. "What're you going to say?"

Natalie reached into her pocket and pulled out a few crumpled dollar bills.

"That I want to buy some eggs."

CHAPTER 40

"It's funny." Angie McBride shook her head as she poured iced tea for the teenagers who'd come to her door, surprised at herself for inviting them to sit down at all. The girl was very quiet, taking everything in, from the appliances to the kitchen island to the prints on the walls. "When I was a kid, we used to sing hopscotch rhymes about *Cind-er-ella dressed in yell-a*, you know? Around here, it's *Par-ty dress so lil-y white, strang-ler come for you to-night.*"

"I guess I must've missed that one," said the boy.

"Oh, it's real sick. Kids love that stuff, right? Like to spook each other. Around Halloween, we get the usual prank phone calls, toilet paper in the trees."

"This room is great. You've done so much with it," the girl said. Her gaze never stopped traveling.

"Well, thanks. You two want the ten-cent tour?" *Now why did you just offer that?* she wondered.

As they went from room to room, the boy and girl hung on every word she said about her family moving in, turning it back into a working farm.

"It doesn't bother you to live here, knowing what happened?" the girl said.

"Eh. Houses are meant to be lived in. The real estate agent was very up-front about it. Hell, it's silly. Plenty of people around here own places old as this one—they don't think a few folks kicked the bucket in those rooms? With influenza and cholera and who knows what else, women having ten kids and losing five? Murder's nasty, but it ain't new. It just so happens that everybody around here knows about ours."

She showed them out.

"You have a wonderful home," the girl said, and to Angie's bewilderment, the child was almost in tears. She had pale gray eyes like chips of ice. "I'm glad nice people are taking care of it." She reached out and touched Angie's hand. Something cold and electric passed between them, and then was gone.

Angie murmured thanks, watching them set their glasses on the countertop and head for the door.

"Honey, wait."

The girl turned back to her, wide-eyed.

Angie picked up the cardboard container. "Don't forget your eggs."

Angie went to the dooryard and watched them drive away. They slowed down to look at the cows, then accelerated again and disappeared from sight.

Angie couldn't seem to get the warmth back in her hands, and suffered from a chill the rest of the day. It was almost, she told her husband later with forced humor, as if the girl had been a ghost herself.

ACKNOWLEDGMENTS

Many thanks to Melissa Kim and the team at Islandport Press for giving an unknown YA author an incredible opportunity; to Anne Romans, a superior library director and friend; Ellen Potter, whose editorial advice was priceless; and to my husband Darren, whose faith never wavered.

AUTHOR INTERVIEW

Q: **What inspired** *The Door to January?*
A: My surroundings. I've lived in Maine my entire life, and my childhood home was a 1700s cape. The barn and outbuildings were gone by the time we moved in, but my parents encouraged an interest in the original residents and what the property looked like centuries before. In New England, the mystery of the past is everywhere, and I tried to tap into that while writing the book.

Q: **What kind of research did you do for your book?**
A: Thomas Hubka's *Big House, Little House, Back House, Barn* was essential—the photos and diagrams helped me understand the layout of a Georgian Colonial. *The Great Steel Pier* by Peter Dow Bachelder was also vital in writing the 1948 flashback to the Old Orchard Beach Pier. Many of the smaller details of 1940s life, such as slang and dress, came from my own interest; I enjoy films and novels that highlight that era.

Q: **Bullying plays a large part in the modern-day sequences of** *The Door to January.* **Is any of it based on your own experiences?**
A: I was lucky to be a middle-of-the-road kid, not cool but not exactly a target, either. That said, I remember how brutal teen social politics can be, how you can find yourself following a crowd and later regret your actions; or wish you'd spoken up against something you knew was wrong.

Q: **Do you believe in ghosts?**

A: I want to believe. I've yet to see a ghost myself, though I did experience something strange in my parents' house as a teenager. We heard the sound of the back door opening and closing, followed by a man's footsteps. When my dad went to check out the noise, nobody was there. You can find the beginnings of *The Door to January* in that!

ABOUT THE AUTHOR

Growing up in rural Maine led Gillian French to believe that the mystery of the past is all around. She uses her surroundings as a setting for her dark stories that often have a creepy twist. Her short fiction has appeared in various publications and anthologies, and her YA novels include *Grit, The Lies They Tell,* and *The Missing Season*. She lives with her husband and two sons in Maine, where she is perpetually at work on her next novel.